THRESHOLDS

WITHDRAWN

Books by
NINA KIRIKI HOFFMAN

NINA KIRIKI HOFFMAN

THRESHOLDS

VIKING
An Imprint of Penguin Group (USA) Inc.

VIKING
Published by Penguin Group
Penguin Young Readers Group, 345 Hudson Street, New York, New York 10014, U.S.A.
Penguin Group (Canada), 90 Eglinton Avenue East, Suite 700, Toronto, Ontario, Canada M4P 2Y3
(a division of Pearson Penguin Canada Inc.)
Penguin Books Ltd, 80 Strand, London WC2R 0RL, England
Penguin Ireland, 25 St Stephen's Green, Dublin 2, Ireland (a division of Penguin Books Ltd)
Penguin Group (Australia), 250 Camberwell Road, Camberwell, Victoria 3124, Australia
(a division of Pearson Australia Group Pty Ltd)
Penguin Books India Pvt Ltd, 11 Community Centre, Panchsheel Park, New Delhi – 110 017, India
Penguin Group (NZ), 67 Apollo Drive, Rosedale, North Shore 0632, New Zealand
(a division of Pearson New Zealand Ltd)
Penguin Books (South Africa) (Pty) Ltd, 24 Sturdee Avenue, Rosebank, Johannesburg 2196, South Africa

Penguin Books Ltd, Registered Offices: 80 Strand, London WC2R 0RL, England

First published in the U.S.A. by Viking, a member of Penguin Young Readers Group, 2010

1   3   5   7   9   10   8   6   4   2

LIBRARY OF CONGRESS CATALOGING-IN-PUBLICATION DATA IS AVAILABLE
ISBN: 978-0-670-06319-2

Printed in U.S.A.   Set in Minion   Book design by Jim Hoover

To Liberty HS and Marga G—thanks for talking to me about your middle school experiences. To Amanda D and Aerin L—thanks for being inspirational twelve-year-olds (yeah, I know you're not twelve anymore). To Ashton M, wizard, ghoul, and archaeologist: always an inspiration. To Emily M and Flora W and their writing dreams: See you in print! ☺

THRESHOLDS

* ONE *

It was Maya's second week in the new house. She woke a couple of hours after she had gone to sleep, wondering what had alerted her. A sound? A movement?

A rush of wings?

She stared up at the new ceiling, with its splash of orange light from the streetlamp outside. A light breeze shifted the curtains in the open window, changing the shape of the light: a tyrannosaurus head, an island, an angel.

Dad planned to get screens for the upstairs windows, but with all the furniture shuffling, box unpacking, and register-ing three kids in new schools, screens hadn't happened yet.

Had something come into her room?

Her new window faced the huge apartment house next door, with its mix of architectural styles. It was about four stories tall, as near as she could tell; there were lots of roof bits sticking up that might contain another story's worth of assorted attics.

A porch wrapped around the ground floor, and balconies interrupted different levels of the upstairs. A variety of doors opened onto the porch; some parts of the porch hosted wicker furniture; some, bench swings; some, jungly assortments of plants.

Lawn covered the ground between the Janus House Apartments and Maya's house, with no fence or hedge to interrupt it.

The new neighbors fascinated Maya. Their clothes didn't come from any catalog or store she knew about. Some of them looked like they had stepped out of the past, some as though they came from an unimagined future, and some as though they came from some European country where people cobbled outfits together from things found in attics.

Sometimes people came out of the building and sat on the porch or the lawn. Older kids played games that involved nets and feathered things and rackets, or balls and mallets. Sometimes they and the younger children played hide-and-seek. From her upstairs room, in the shadow of her curtain, Maya watched, seeing where the hidden were, and how the searchers searched.

One night, a bunch of the people brought out chairs and musical instruments and played a concert, with some singing, though the words were lost over the short distance between the houses. She could tell they were excellent harmonizers. The music was unlike anything Maya had heard on the radio or online or in her living room on Saturday night Music Night, though she could tell some of the instruments were stringed, some wind, some percussion. She sat at her desk, looked out the window, and sketched people and their instruments, none of which seemed entirely normal. One of the melodies stuck in her brain for days.

Maya was going to start the first day of seventh grade in a new school in the morning, and she wondered if any of the neighbor kids would be in her class. Her whole family was starting over: her older sister, Candra, was heading to high school, along with their father, who taught history; her little brother, Peter, and their mother would go to the elementary school, where their mother taught fourth grade.

The Andersens had moved from a small town in Idaho to Spores Ferry, Oregon, so everybody could get a new start, especially Maya. Maya's best friend, Stephanie, had died in the spring.

Everybody had loved freckled, ginger-haired Stephanie, who had been stocky and strong, ready for adventure, and always anticipating wonders. The illness that ate her up made them all mad. Where was the superhero with the antidote, the genie with the wish, the good fairy with the magic ointment to make it go away? None of them had showed up, though Stephanie had been telling Maya stories about them all since she learned to talk.

The doctors put Stephanie through radiation and chemotherapy, and that still hadn't killed the cancer before it killed her.

Everything about the Andersens' house in Idaho had reminded Maya of Stephanie; they had hidden together in that closet, slid down that banister and fallen in a laughing heap at the bottom, sung Christmas carols around that piano with the rest of Maya's family. They had known each other all their lives.

Stephanie had always been sure something surprising and wonderful would arrive soon, and even though it seldom did, Maya loved the anticipation Stephanie was so good at drumming up. Stephanie had hoped for a miracle almost up until the end, so Maya had hoped, too.

That was one of the things that made Maya maddest, after Steph died.

Maya missed Stephanie's stories. Stephanie found fairies in the fields, dragons in the ditches, ghosts in clouds and closets and attics, witches in the hedges. Stephanie had spun stories as she walked through the world, and Maya had illustrated them.

After Stephanie died, Maya had spent a melancholy spring and summer. Some days she couldn't even get out of bed. Her parents sent her to a counselor, and that had helped, but sadness still overwhelmed her now and then. Anything could trigger a memory.

She searched for Stephanie's ghost in all their old haunts— at the swimming pool and the mall and even at the elementary school, where they had gone to shoot baskets after school was out, and penciled charms and curses in secret code on the backs of some of the rocks at the edge of the playground. Stephanie was everywhere and nowhere.

Without Stephanie, nothing was bright. Nothing was funny. Nothing mattered.

Budget cuts at the Idaho high school where Maya's father taught meant he'd have to take a big pay cut to stay there, so he had begun job hunting even before Stephanie died. He and Mom both found good jobs in Spores Ferry that summer, provided they could move right away. Mom said the family was ready for a change after spending seventeen years in the same place, but Candra was sure angry about the move—she had a lot of friends she was leaving behind.

Maya hadn't wanted to leave Catspaw, either. At the same time, she didn't want to stay there. Everything and everywhere in Catspaw reminded her of Stephanie, and sometimes she liked that, but mostly it meant she was sad all the time.

Maya stared up at the orange blotch of shifting light on her new ceiling, wondering about wings. Again she heard a faint flutter and a faraway jingle.

After Stephanie died, Maya had drawn through sketchbook after sketchbook, mostly pictures of Stephanie. The curve of Stephanie's freckled cheek, her kinky hair like a perpetual explosion around her head, her uneven smile, her lowered lashes as she looked down at something in her hands, a baby bird or a rabbit or a lizard, her long fingers gently cupped around something alive. The dome of Stephanie's bald head after chemo made her hair fall out—how much brighter her eyes had been then, even on the days when she was so sick . . . Maya crosshatched and charcoaled and penciled, making Stephanie shapes rise from the page by darkening the space around them.

Since the move, Dad had challenged Maya to draw other things. He took her out sketching. They sat at outdoor tables at coffee shops, Dad with his sketchpad, Maya with hers. They drew passersby and people sitting at other tables. They went to museums and art galleries to look at other people's art. He took her to parks and hiking trails, along with her brother and sister, who went on ahead while Dad and Maya stopped to sketch, though Maya was more interested in drawing people than places.

To draw the worlds Stephanie had made up, Maya had needed trees and plants—sometimes flowers and leaves, sometimes a ragged line of forest across a meadow. She still drew things that would have come in handy if Stephanie were with her, inventing.

Sometimes the sketch trips worked. Sometimes Maya tuned in to the nearby world and forgot the past. Sometimes when she was in the middle of capturing the world around her, she thought about how useful this was going to be when she and Stephanie got together to make up another world. Then she remembered Stephanie was gone, and she felt guilty for not remembering it all the time.

She felt guilty being in a new place, too. Stephanie was nowhere in this new/old house, except in the photographs Maya had put on her dresser, in a few sketches Maya had tacked to the wall, and in the celadon pottery bowl on the desk, full of rough garnets Maya and Stephanie had found in a creek in northern Idaho on a camping trip.

Maya felt herself letting go of Stephanie sometimes. Mom said that was a good thing, but it felt like a betrayal.

"If no one remembers her, it'll be like she was never here," Maya told her mother.

"You're not going to forget, and neither are we. Neither is her family. She won't be erased, honey." Mom had hugged Maya.

Sometimes Maya believed her.

The curtains fluttered. A winged shadow flickered across the orange patch, the largest moth Maya had ever seen.

Or was it a moth? Maya heard a hummingbird hum of wings, and tiny, distant jingling noises, like glass wind chimes. She smelled a spicy cinnamon/carnation scent.

Not a moth.

A fairy.

It hovered, gilded in orange light, its wings a blur of motion. It came to rest on the dresser next to the picture of Maya and Stephanie at five, riding ponies at the county fair. It was about eight inches tall, dark skinned, slender, and smooth, an elongated human shape with bunches of wings fanning out from its back. The wings didn't look like angels' or dragon-flies' or bats'—more like feather dusters.

Maya closed her eyes, wondering if she was dreaming the strange small shadowy shape, its face and form half lit by the streetlamp, iridescence blurring its wings. She opened her eyes quickly, afraid the vision would be gone. Who cared if it was a dream? She could study it. She could draw it. Her hand edged toward the sketchpad she kept on her bedside table.

If only Stephanie were here to see. All their lives they had longed for magic, and finally, when it was too late, here it was. Maya's throat tightened.

She could draw it, the way she had been drawing every-thing—keeping a record for someone who would never see it. But what if she startled the fairy, and it left? She stilled.

The fairy turned its face toward her, sliding into shadow. Its eyes had a faint orange-yellow glow. It blinked. Maya held her breath.

It made a small purring sound that ended in a question mark.

Its wings beat faster. It lifted from the dresser and came toward the bed.

Maya froze. The spicy scent grew stronger, and the windchimey sounds. She heard the fluttering beat of its wings.

It landed on her bed with a less-than-graceful thump, then stalked across the bumpy chenille bedspread toward her, its head turning, its large glowing eyes scanning Maya's sideways form under the blanket, a mountain range to something the size of a fairy, or at least a chain of hills.

Maya couldn't hold her breath any longer. She let it out slowly and opened her mouth to suck in more spicy-tasting air, even though she was afraid she'd scare the fairy away.

It paused. She heard a sniffing sound. Its wings rustled.

Then it stepped closer and leaned against her stomach. It groomed its wings, settled them so they were folded tight like collapsed fans against its back, knelt, turned around three times with muffled jingling, and curled into a ball. It sighed a tiny sigh and went to sleep.

It made a small warm weight against her stomach. Maya stared and stared, telling her hands to remember the sights her eyes collected. Nothing else happened.

Trapped by her desire to keep the fairy near her, afraid to move, Maya lay tense, but eventually she couldn't keep her body locked up any longer. She relaxed. The fairy stayed still.

Maya fell asleep.

* TWO *

Maya woke with a start. Sunlight spotted the floor, and her alarm was about to go off.

She sat up, switched off the alarm, and searched for the fairy. It was gone. A glittering imprint on the fuzzy chenille bedspread was all that was left.

Maya grabbed her pad and pencil and went to work, outlining as many views of the fairy as she could remember: It hovered in the air, its wings quick scattered strokes. It stood in half-light by the photos on the dresser. It curled like a kitten against her stomach.

After she had four pages of fairy sketches, she pressed her hand against the golden dust on her bedspread. Her palm tingled. She lifted it and looked at the pale glow. Proof that she hadn't dreamed it? Or just dust?

She rubbed her palms against each other and stared down at her gleaming, tingling hands. Nobody would believe this. Her seventeen-year-old sister Candra was too logical. Ten-year-old Peter . . . he might believe, but what would he do about it? He loved catching things—tadpoles, frogs, lizards, snakes, grasshoppers—anything he could put in a jar with airholes punched through the top. He might haunt her room, hoping for another fairy visit. No. She wasn't ready to share such an awesome secret with Peter the Pest.

Her practical parents? Forget it. They'd been telling her and Stephanie "There's no such thing as . . ." since she was three.

Stephanie would have understood. Maya went to her dresser and looked at the most recent photo of Stephanie she had, Steph's last school picture before she got sick. That freckled smile, so wide. "Guess what," Maya whispered. Stephanie's smile didn't change.

A flash of anger shot through Maya. She turned away. This was a secret she could hug to herself, a charm to carry through the day ahead.

She went back to the bed and sat beside the gold-dusted

spot on the bedspread. She touched one hand to the hollow of her throat, transferring the skin-buzzing sensation there. Then she wiped both hands through the remaining dust on the bedspread and brushed one hand across the best page she'd drawn. The dust tinted her images of the fairy with gold. She lifted the book to her nose and sniffed. That spicy cinnamon/carnation scent. Was fairy dust the fairy equivalent of human sweat? Much more fun to play with, anyway, and definitely better smelling.

Knocks sounded on her door. "Maya!" cried Peter. "Mom sent me to wake you up! Why can't you use an alarm clock like everybody else? We're almost done with breakfast!" He opened the door and came in. "Oh, good. You're awake. Get up!"

"You *know* I hate it when you open the door before I say come in!" She glanced toward the clock. It was seven thirty, and she was due at school by eight fifteen. "Gah," she cried, erupting from her bed and scattering sketchbook and pencils on the floor. "Get out of here!"

Peter left, slamming the door behind him.

Maya went to the chair where she had laid out her clothes for the first day of school: underwear, socks, jeans, an orange T-shirt that darkened to red at the hem, and a gray hoodie with purple lining. She slithered out of her nightgown and into the clothes, then stuffed her sketchpad and pencils into the prepacked backpack with all her other school supplies. She dashed downstairs.

The new kitchen was big enough for Mom and Dad to both stand in front of the stove at once. Their old kitchen had been tiny and dark and couldn't hold more than three people at the same time. There was a table in the new kitchen that three kids and two parents could sit at without jamming elbows.

Sully, their golden retriever, lay on the floor by the freezer. He thumped his tail twice when Maya arrived.

Maya's brother and sister sat at the table, eating. She and her siblings had the same coloring: silver-blond hair and seawater gray-green eyes. In that, they resembled their father. Candra was tall and thin like their father, but Peter and Maya were shorter and denser, like their mom, who looked solid and strong. Mom's hair was light brown, and she had maple syrup-colored eyes and a strong, square face.

"Oatmeal or scrambled eggs?" Mom asked Maya as Maya sat at the table.

"Oatmeal, please."

Mom scooped up a bowlful and set it in front of

Maya. "Eat fast," she said. "You're later than usual today."

"I had this dream—"

"Eat," said Candra. "Don't talk. You want to make Mom and Dad late on their first day?"

Maya dumped brown sugar, raisins, and milk on her oatmeal, then shoveled it in her mouth.

Dad set a brown bag, its top folded over, next to her bowl. "Lunch," he said. "From now on, you're responsible for making your own lunch, all right?"

"Thanks, Dad." She stuffed the lunch into her backpack. "Hey, squirt," she said to Peter, "thanks for getting me up."

"Yeah. Okay for today, but you gotta take care of yourself now, Maya."

"I know," she said.

"Have a great first day, everyone," Dad said. "You ready, Candra?"

Candra rose and put on her black leather jacket and her pack. She followed Dad out.

Peter stood up in a rush, gave Sully a big hug, and grabbed his pack. "Do you think my teacher will have animals, Mom?"

"I know he will. I've already seen your classroom." Maya's mother turned to her. "Lock the door when you go out. This isn't small-town Idaho. Take care of yourself, sweetie. See you after school." She herded Peter out the back door toward the car.

Maya was heading to school by herself for the first time. Hoover Middle School was close enough to walk to. She felt strange and forlorn, alone in the new house, abandoned by everybody except Sully, who was scarfing up something someone had dropped on the floor—with any luck, food. Sully had a history of inappropriate eating, with subsequent throwing up in inconvenient and newly slippery places.

Last year, B.C.—Before Cancer—Stephanie had spent the night at Maya's before the first day of school. They had headed to sixth grade together the next morning, wearing matching black headbands with crystal stars on them, and when they got to their classroom, they knew all the other kids already. "It's the witch twins," one of the kids said, and other kids laughed. So did Stephanie. "Watch it," Stephanie had said, "or I'll put spells on you all!"

Maya let Sully slurp up the dregs of her oatmeal before she put him in the backyard with a big bowl of water for the day. She left the house by the front door, letting it lock behind her before she checked her pockets and discovered she hadn't remembered her key.

By the time she got home, someone else would be there, probably Mom and Peter, and they could let her in.

Sully barked from the backyard as Maya headed down the street past the Janus House Apartments. She barked back. Just then, three kids slammed out of the Janus's big front door.

✳ THREE ✳

A tall girl and boy led the way across the front porch, followed by a shorter boy. Maya hoped they hadn't heard her barking at her dog.

Stephanie would have laughed at Maya if she were here. She never cared what other people thought.

"You are such a *scrunt*," the tall, dark boy said to the girl as they came closer, "such a *smitch*! When will you ever learn?"

"Shut up," the girl said. She had long, curly, dark brown hair and an oval face with dark brows, blue eyes, and a generous mouth. Her skin was pale. She wore a black spiderweb shawl over an embroidered blouse, a ruffly maroon calf-length skirt, and tall red boots. She had a tapestry bag slung over one shoulder. A charm bracelet dangled from her right wrist. She looked more like somebody off on a quest in a fairy tale than a middle school student.

She was frowning. Maya wondered what her smile would look like.

Maya's fingers itched to draw her.

"How could you screw up at a time like this?" asked the tall boy in a mean voice. "Haven't you been watching the message traffic? Something big and bad is going on. We have to be extra careful right now."

The tall boy wore black jeans and a black long-sleeved shirt. His straight, ragged, black hair hung down to his shoulders and covered half his face. The part of his face Maya could see looked caramel brown and handsome, but frowny. The eye she could see was honey brown.

Maya wanted to draw him too, for different reasons.

"How could you leave the door open with a traveler in the tea room?" he asked.

"I went to get her some nectar," said the gypsy girl. "I didn't know she'd leave."

The shorter boy's skin was the gold of onion skins. He was wearing jeans and a green T-shirt and a big black and red backpack. He looked way too normal to live at Janus House.

He saw Maya and nudged the other boy. "Hey," he said.

"Never leave the door to the tea room open!" the tall boy repeated. "Don't you know your basic wards? What's the matter with you?"

"Leave me alone." The girl shifted her shoulders, turning her face away from him. "I made a mistake. I get it. We found her again. Give me a break!"

The shorter boy tugged the taller one's sleeve. "Hey," he said, a little louder.

"At a time like this, when things are missing and nobody knows where, when everybody's already worried, you can't make stupid mistakes," the taller boy went on. "She was gone for hours!"

"Hey, Rowan, *shut up*," said the shorter boy.

Rowan brushed the hair out of his face and gave the shorter boy a glare. The shorter boy jerked his head toward Maya.

Rowan looked up. Saw Maya. Glared some more, this time at her. She could almost feel the heat in his gaze.

"Hi, there," Maya said. She finger-waved.

The girl smiled at her as the three of them came closer. Nice smile. Maya felt a sudden rush of hope. Maybe she'd found a new friend. Just as quickly, she felt a rush of shame. She already had a best friend . . . well, no, not anymore.

"Hello," said the gypsy girl. "We were just talking about pet mice."

Mice? Nectar for mice? A tea room for mice?

Maya's heart beat faster. She realized they had been discussing a missing person, and they wanted to keep it quiet.

What if their missing person was . . . her fairy? The nectar would fit, but she wasn't sure about the tea room. Or the big and bad thing, or things missing. If they *were* talking about her fairy, what else might they believe in or know about?

On the other hand . . . *mice*? Okay, a dodge, and not a very convincing one. Secrets. Maya was happy with the prospect of secrets.

"You have mice?" Maya said. "We have a dog. We just moved into the house next door." She pointed.

"Oh?" said the girl. She smelled faintly of incense. "You're in the Spring House? I'm Gwenda, and these are my cousins, Rowan"—Gwenda pointed to the taller boy—"and Benjamin."

"Maya," Maya said, wondering if they would shake hands. Gwenda didn't stick out her hand, so Maya didn't, either. "Nice to meet you. My little brother really likes animals. I'm sure he'd like to see your mice."

"We don't—" Rowan began in a cold voice.

"The mice are kind of shy," said Benjamin. "Maybe later."

"Cool." Maya checked her watch. "Oh, no!"

"What time is it?" Gwenda asked.

"Eight." Homeroom started at 8:15. Maya didn't want to be late on her first day in a new school. She tightened her backpack straps and ran.

Their footsteps followed her.

Benjamin caught up with her. "Hoover Middle School?"

"Yeah. Seventh grade. You?"

"Same," he said as they ran. "All three of us."

Hope stirred in her chest again. "Maybe we'll have some classes together."

"Probably. Are you—" He paused and panted. They kept running. "Are you a traveler? Are you *chikuvny*?"

"Huh?" She wasn't sure she'd heard him right.

"Oh. Nothing." He flashed her a sweet smile.

He looked so nice she wanted to trust him. "Do you believe—" *in fairies?* No, she couldn't say that to somebody out of the blue.

Just because they talked about visitors in their tea room didn't mean they were strange. Old-fashioned or English, maybe, but not necessarily hosts to fairies.

She peeked at Benjamin. He looked like a perfectly normal kid.

She glanced over her shoulder at Rowan and Gwenda. Nope. Not exactly normal. Rowan loped easily where Maya was puffing, but it wasn't just his athleticism that impressed her. There was definitely something strange about him.

Gwenda looked like a gypsy.

Maya wondered if they would let her paint them or if she would have to do it on the sly.

"Do I believe what?" Benjamin asked when Maya had been quiet for half a block.

"Do you believe we'll make it in time?"

"It's the first day. Everything's nuts on the first day," he said. "Even if we're a little late, we should be okay."

Cars sped by them on Passage Street, pulled into the loop of road that led past the front of the yellow brick complex that was Hoover Middle School, and dropped off kids. A couple of empty school buses pulled out of the side lot.

Oregon kids looked a lot like kids from her old school in Idaho. She glanced down at her clothes and at other people's. Gwenda's dress was the most interesting outfit.

Maya slowed as they came even with the front entrance, and so did Benjamin. Rowan and Gwenda moved up beside her. Maya waited for new-kid chemistry to kick in, for all the powers that were to notice her, judge her, decide whether to snub her for the rest of the year or give her a break. She'd seen it happen to new kids at her old school. This was the first time she was the new kid. The first time she didn't know a soul at school.

Then she thought: *Hey. I'm not alone.*

She didn't even know these kids, but she was already in a group.

She felt warm and happy.

For about two seconds.

"Hey! Tovah! How was summer camp?" Gwenda cried, and ran off to talk to a short girl with masses of dark crinkly hair.

Rowan stalked past Maya toward the front entrance, not looking at anybody.

She glanced at Benjamin. Was he going to take off, too? "Gee," she said, "is he always that friendly?"

Benjamin smiled. "You bet."

She pulled out her class schedule. "I have Mr. Ferrell for homeroom first period. Room M44."

Benjamin said, "Me, too."

"What does 'M' mean?" she asked.

"M is the main building. This place is kind of a maze. Follow me." Benjamin headed toward the front entrance.

"Cool," she said. A boy she already knew was in her homeroom, and he lived right next door. Plus, he'd agreed to be her native guide without her even asking.

They pushed inside and entered a long, low-ceilinged hall where the odor of disinfectant and various people scents clashed. Kids crowded the hallway, talking fast and hard. Banks of lockers lined the walls, interspersed with doorways. Fluorescent lights ran down the center of the ceiling and made everyone look like they were in a bad movie.

An ear-battering bell rang down the hallway, cutting through conversations. "First bell. Five minutes," Benjamin said. "This way."

Unfortunately, Benjamin was short, and he was going fast. She lost him after one turn.

She jumped up and down, trying to see over people's heads. No luck. She couldn't find him in the sea of heads and backpacks.

She touched a tall girl's sleeve and said, "Room M44?"

"That way." The girl pointed to another hallway. "Take a right."

"Thanks." Maya rounded the corner and jumped up to

search for Benjamin's dark head again. When she came down, she slammed into a guy she hadn't even noticed. She grabbed his arm to keep herself from falling.

She stared up into his dark blue eyes. He had short, wavy, auburn hair and a spatter of dark freckles across his face. He was a head taller than she was, and pretty muscular. This was easy to tell, because his gray T-shirt didn't have any sleeves.

He smelled . . . strange. Sour, like maybe he'd just been sick. Shadows framed his eyes, and his skin was pale under his freckles. He radiated heat.

Her hand tingled and pulsed against the bare skin of his upper arm.

"Chikuvny," whispered the boy.

✳ FOUR ✳

"Huh?" Maya said.

"*Chikuvny,*" he said.

Benjamin had asked her if she were *chikuvny.* What the heck was it, and what made these guys think it had anything to do with her? "Sorry, no," she said.

"Where is the portal?" the boy asked. He gripped her wrists. His hands felt fever hot. His intensity scared her.

"What portal? I don't know what you're talking about."

"I must find the portal." Sweat streaked his face.

"You're sick," she said. "Maybe you should see the nurse." She glanced around. She wished she had a map of the school. She had no idea where the infirmary was, or anything else.

"No. No nurses. No doctors," he said. "I only need a portal."

"And I need to find M44. Do you know where that is?"

He shook his head.

"I have to go," she said, trying to break his grip. He was way strong for a sick guy.

He didn't let go of her wrists, just stared into her eyes.

She looked away. Kids were clearing the halls, funneling into classrooms.

Should she yell for help?

Sick Boy finally released her.

She rubbed her wrists and ran down the hall, then glanced back. He stood there, swaying like he was going to fall, still staring at her.

She was sure he needed help. She had no idea how to get it for him, and she didn't want to get near him. She didn't want him to grab her again.

Second bell rang.

She ran, checked room numbers, then glanced back again.

He had disappeared.

Nothing she could do now.

She found her homeroom at the end of the hall. Most of the desks were taken by people who already knew and were talking to each other. There were some empty seats in the front row, but who wanted to sit there?

Gwenda and Benjamin were in the back row, and there were empty desks all around them. Maya took the desk beside Benjamin and dug into her backpack.

Benjamin smiled at her, which was a relief.

"Guess what just happened?" she said.

"Settle down, settle down." The teacher, a guy with carroty orange hair and a big red mustache, wrote MR. FERRELL on the green board. "Time for check-in." He held up a computer printout. "Do we have an Albert Brandy here?"

A few girls giggled. One of them raised her hand. "I'm Brandy Albert," she said.

Mr. Ferrell made a mark on his sheet and called more names.

Gwenda's last name was Janus. Benjamin's last name was Porta. When Mr. Ferrell got to them, kids turned in their chairs and glanced at them with strange expressions. Some muttered to each other.

Maya guessed the empty desks around Gwenda and Benjamin should have clued her in.

Maybe she'd picked the wrong friends.

She checked out the other kids. None of them looked as interesting, though some of them looked nice. Brandy sat with three other girls. All four of them had the same style of ponytail streaming from the left sides of their heads, though their hair color ranged from blonde to black. They were all chewing gum, too. No way she wanted to be part of the Brandy Brigade.

Mr. Ferrell finished attendance and said, "Are you in the seats you want for the rest of the semester? I'm going to make a seating chart, so be sure."

"You could still move," Benjamin whispered to Maya.

"I like it here," she whispered back.

A couple of kids shifted in their seats and looked around. One girl moved back a row.

"Okay. I'm charting you now," said Mr. Ferrell. "I may have to ask for names again. Help me out."

Maya pulled out her class schedule and showed it to Benjamin. "You have any of these classes?" she whispered.

Before he could answer, the door opened and a boy with long, ragged blond hair slouched in. He was taller than anybody else in class. He looked like he worked out with weights. The knees of his worn jeans had giant holes in them, and his white T-shirt was marked with dark stains, as though he'd dunked his hands in grease and then wiped them on it.

"Mr. Finnegan," said Mr. Ferrell in a mean voice. "So nice of you to grace us with your presence."

The boy burped, a long, melodious one, which made everybody laugh. He shambled toward Maya and collapsed into the desk next to hers, yawning. He didn't have a backpack or anything, not even a pencil. He smelled like fried bacon.

"So here's how it works at Hoover," said Mr. Ferrell, and he launched into a monologue.

Benjamin tapped *Spanish* and *Art* on Maya's class grid.

Oh, good. She sat back, then leaned forward. She had all kinds of questions.

She got her binder out of her backpack. On a fresh piece of paper, she wrote:

What's cheekoovnee?

After checking to make sure Mr. Ferrell wasn't looking, she edged the paper over onto Benjamin's desk.

He looked at the note, then glanced at Gwenda, who was watching them. She leaned forward and scanned the note. She sat back, her eyebrows up.

Benjamin wrote on the paper, showed it to Gwenda, who nodded, and passed it back to Maya.

Chikuvny. It's a kind of perfume.

This was *so* not what she expected.

I don't wear perfume.

You smell good anyway.

She cocked her head sideways to see if she could get a different view of Benjamin. He had to be joking.

She sniffed the back of her hand, still watching him. He shrugged, half smiled. She sniffed her palm.

Carnation and cinnamon.

Fairy dust! Tiny gold glints still gleamed in the lines of her palms, though she had washed her hands before breakfast. Or had she?

Was there really a strong enough scent left to make two different guys accuse her of wearing some perfume she'd never heard of? She stared at Benjamin, and he stared back with dark, serious eyes.

Maybe fairy dust had made her hand tingle when she touched the guy in the hall.

She reached toward Benjamin, wondering what would happen if she touched *him*. Then she thought, *No, this is way too weird.*

He held out a hand, though. Her hand moved toward it.

"Miss Andersen!" yelled Mr. Ferrell from the front of the room.

She jerked her hand back.

Everybody turned to stare at her.

* FIVE *

"Yes, Mr. Ferrell?" Maya said.

"You should know my policy on note passing. When I observe notes being passed, I confiscate them and read them aloud to the whole class. Since this is your first offense, I'll let you off with a warning, but I want everyone in this room to understand I'm serious about this."

She felt her face heat. She stared down at her notebook.

The blond guy on her other side grabbed the note off her desk, wadded it up, and stuck it in his mouth.

"Mr. Finnegan!" Mr. Ferrell yelled.

The boy chewed.

Mr. Ferrell sighed. "Welcome back, Mr. Finnegan. It

seems you haven't changed since the last time you were in seventh grade."

The boy swallowed. "Thanks, dude." He turned to Maya, raised his eyebrows, and smiled.

She tried to smile back at him, but the truth was, she was mad. She'd been let off with a warning. She could have kept her note. She liked how Benjamin wrote: his letters were spiky and close together, but they were all there. Her first note. If something dire happened and nobody liked her after this morning, it might be her last friendly communication at Hoover.

"One more stunt like that, Mr. Finnegan, and you will visit Principal Clark," Mr. Ferrell said. "Does anyone have any legitimate questions?"

Maya raised her hand.

"Miss Andersen," said Mr. Ferrell.

"Is there a map of the school? I got lost trying to find this room."

"You were supposed to get a map at Orientation," he said.

"We didn't move to town in time for Orientation."

"Oh, that's right." Mr. Ferrell riffled through a short stack of papers. "I have a note here from the counselor's office.

You're to stop by at the end of the day to pick up some paper-work from Mrs. Boleslav. She'll give you a map."

Great. She got to spend her first day without a map.

The big blond note-eating kid next to her burped and said, "I'll show you around."

"Gee," she said. "Thanks."

"No prob, dudette."

Dudette?

She glanced at Benjamin and Gwenda, wondering if they would save her from the blond kid. Benjamin waggled his eyebrows and shrugged.

"What's your name, anyway?" she whispered to her new guide. "Or do you want me to call you Mr. Finnegan?"

"Travis," he whispered back. "Who are you?"

"Maya," she said.

"Nice to meet you." Travis smiled, yawned, and slumped in his seat, then closed his eyes and started snoring. It sounded really fake. How could anybody fall asleep that fast? She leaned forward and studied his face. All the muscles had gone slack, so maybe insta-nap was one of his superpowers.

"Come up when I call your name and I'll give you your locker assignment. You're responsible for your own locks," Mr. Ferrell said.

While she waited for Mr. Ferrell to call her name, she doodled in her notebook. A picture of Travis's sleeping face. Quick sketches of Gwenda and Benjamin—then she flipped the page over so they wouldn't see. Another of Gwenda and Rowan fighting, drawn from memory. A sketch of Rowan's face, obscured by hair. She was going to start folders of sketches of the new neighbors when she got home. Sketch them anytime she could, then move on to paint at some point.

She drew the fairy again. If she drew her enough, maybe she'd get her right.

Mr. Ferrell said, "Janus." Gwenda got up, went to the front of the room, and came back.

The fairy had definitely had arms *and* wings. Maybe she was more like a bug than a person. Maya had books on human and animal anatomy, but she hadn't studied bugs yet. If the fairy was just something she'd made up, there weren't any rules anyway. Why not give her eight limbs?

Because that wasn't what Maya had seen.

Benjamin poked her shoulder. Startled, she drew a long line across her picture.

"Sorry," he whispered. "You're supposed to go up front now."

She closed her notebook and went up.

At the front desk, Mr. Ferrell said, "What's your next class? I can give you directions."

"Language arts block. With Ms. Caras. Room L38."

He got out a piece of paper and sketched a map that involved lots of squares and some numbers. "Longfellow 38. We're here in the main building," he said, making an *X*. "Ms. Caras's class is in this building over here, Longfellow."

"Thanks," she said.

"You're welcome. Sorry I came down on you so hard about the notes, but I need to make a few things clear from the start every year, and you presented me with an opportunity."

She smiled and shrugged, took the map, and went back to her desk.

Her notebook was open to a picture of the fairy.

She knew she hadn't left it that way.

∗ SIX ∗

She glanced at Benjamin. His nose was buried in a book. Beyond him, Gwenda stared off into space and tapped out a rhythm with her pencil.

Travis still looked asleep, though he wasn't making overdone snoring noises anymore.

Maya sat and flipped the page over in her notebook. She set her new school map on top of it.

If there was one thing she hated, it was someone snooping in her stuff. They had had lots of arguments about this at home, at least until Peter reached the civilized age of eight. Now Dad made him sit in a corner if he invaded her desk or looked in her journal without asking.

Her stomach churned as Mr. Ferrell finished handing out locker assignments.

"Benjamin Porta."

Benjamin went up for his locker, came back, and stared at his book some more.

Should she say something, and maybe risk losing a friend? Not say anything, and not be able to trust? The whole day felt sour.

She sighed. She stared at Benjamin until he glanced up. He closed the book he had been reading. It was a fat, navy blue hardback, battered and waterstained. He flipped it so the title faced down.

If he wanted to keep it secret, it didn't seem fair he was looking at *her* secrets.

She wanted Benjamin to confess.

Red touched his cheeks.

"Was it you?" she whispered.

He studied a United States map on the wall, then nodded without looking at her.

"Well, okay. I don't know you very well yet. I'd appreciate it if you don't look at my things without asking, okay?"

"All right," he mumbled.

Gwenda's eyebrows went up, then down. She wasn't watching them, but Maya could tell she was listening.

Maya flipped the page back. She stared down at her fairy picture. "You like art?" she whispered to Benjamin.

He nodded. "You're really good," he muttered.

"Thanks." She touched her fairy picture and frowned. Again, she wanted to ask if he believed in fairies or magic, but she didn't know how.

She turned the page and drew Dwelf, an elf boy she had made up when she was nine. When all else failed and she was dying of boredom, she drew comic strips of Dwelf's adventures and lost herself in another world. Stephanie had adopted Dwelf, too, and Maya had illustrated the stories Steph made up about him.

This time Dwelf had fan-shaped wings, a first. Often he had no wings, or once in a while, dragonfly wings. She drew glow lines around him.

Benjamin watched. She knew he was watching. Sometimes it made her nervous when people watched her draw, but she didn't mind Benjamin.

Which made zero sense when she thought about it. He'd already betrayed her trust.

The bell rang. People slammed books shut and jumped up. "See you tomorrow," Mr. Ferrell said as everyone rushed out of the room.

She shoved out into the hall past tons of other rushing

students who seemed to know where they were going. She clutched the map Mr. Ferrell had given her. She couldn't tell where the door out of the building was.

Someone tapped her arm. She glanced up. Burpmeister and sleepmeister Travis Finnegan smiled at her. "I can show you where your next class is."

"Oh." She returned his smile. He was trying to help. "While you were asleep, I got a map from Mr. Ferrell." She showed him the map, pointed to the Longfellow building.

"You have Ms. Caras for language arts? Ditto. Come on."

It was easier following him through the halls than getting anywhere on her own. He was as big as an eighth grader, bigger than lots of them, and people moved out of his way.

Besides, who was she to be picky about friends?

Travis had almost the same schedule she did.

He was the first kid she'd met who had actually flunked a grade. They didn't have time for much conversation between classes; she figured out about the flunking by the way teachers welcomed him back to classes he'd taken before. Maya couldn't figure out why he'd flunked anything—he seemed plenty smart.

She followed Travis from language arts to math to the cafeteria for first lunch.

They paused on the threshold until incoming students bumped them inside.

The place smelled like overcooked meat and bad tomato sauce. It was a sprawling, yellow-floored room with long, rectangular tables ringed by plastic chairs. At the far end was a wall of windows.

The hot food buffet was against the left wall. Lots of kids stood in line for school lunches. Others had already staked out tables.

"Did you bring your lunch?" Travis asked.

"Yeah. It's in my pack."

"Great. Where do you want to sit?"

"Um," Maya said, "don't you know anybody else at this school?" She really wanted to find Benjamin and/or Gwenda. She still had lots of questions.

Travis looked at her, eyebrows up.

She could have kicked herself. Here he was being as nice as he could possibly be, and she was trying to get rid of him. What was wrong with her?

"Well, *excuuuuse* me," he said.

"I didn't mean that. I mean, you've been going here

longer than I have. Don't you have friends from last year?" After the words were out of her mouth, she wanted to slap herself. This might be an even worse question.

A flush touched his cheeks. "They're all in eighth grade now."

She thought about how weird that must be. Still in the same school, but all your friends had left you behind. You could see them every day, but what if they wouldn't even talk to you?

"Why don't we—" she began.

"Hey, Travis!" Someone waved from a table full of bigger guys.

"Hey! Jason!" Travis waved back, then glanced at her. "You coming?"

"I want to find Gwenda."

"Suit yourself."

"Thanks for all your help this morning."

He shrugged. "Whatever. If you change your mind, you know where to find me."

"Thanks."

He headed for the table full of boys. She scanned tables, searching for a head of long, curly, brown hair and a black shawl over a pale peasant blouse.

Gwenda sat by a window at a table way over in a corner. Benjamin sat across from her. Rowan and two other girls sat at the table, too. Once again, it appeared the Janus House kids lived on their own little island away from everyone else.

She glanced around, spotted people she had seen in her morning classes, tried to put names with faces. She could pin summer vacation essays on a few people—that had been the first assignment from Ms. Caras, and it had actually helped her find out about the other people in class, including Travis, who wrote about taking a cooking class. Her own essay had been about moving to Oregon.

Jessie. She had been a movie extra. Sarah. Her cat had died. Alex, Guitar Hero. Helen, Mad Scientist Girl who had reported on what happened when you froze eggs and soda pop and microwaved Marshmallow Peeps.

Mad Scientist Girl nodded to her.

Was that an invite?

She smiled at Helen and walked on.

At the Benjamin-and-Gwenda table, everybody had brought their own lunch—in pewter-colored tins, not bags. They ate with strange utensils out of small silvery containers. She didn't recognize anything they were eating.

Rowan and the two girls she hadn't met yet were talking

in low voices, but she couldn't understand a word. They spoke a foreign language.

She paused at the end of the table.

Benjamin glanced up and smiled. "Hey, Maya."

The other four shut up and turned to stare at her.

"You want to sit with us?" Benjamin asked.

"Is that all right? I don't know what the cliques are like here yet. If it's not okay, I'll go away."

"Hey. It's okay. You can join us." He pushed out a chair for her. She sat down beside him. "We're not exactly a clique. We're all family. This is my older sister, Twyla." He pointed to the dark-haired girl on his left. "She's in eighth grade. And this is Rowan's younger sister, Kallie. She's in sixth grade. Guys, this is Maya Andersen. Her family just moved into the Spring House."

"Hi," said Kallie. Like Rowan, she had dark golden skin and straight black hair. Her black eyes weren't so cold, though. She was beautiful. A perfect fairy-tale princess. Maya's fingers twitched.

"You moved?" Twyla said. "You're so lucky! I wish I could move!" Her hair was a mass of frizzy black curls; she had olive skin and honey brown eyes.

"You want to live somewhere else?" Maya asked.

"Anywhere! As long as it's away from"—she jumped, then glared at Rowan across the table—"here."

"Maya moved, and she'll probably move again soon," Rowan said in a cold voice.

"No," Maya said. "I don't think so. The house is perfect. Dad said we could never afford such a great house if it cost what it was really worth. We'll never find a better place."

"Nobody lives in Spring House more than a couple of months, Maya," Twyla said. "We think it's haunted."

"Really? That's so cool!" Maya smiled, then lost her smile. Could ghosts travel? If she was going to be haunted, why not by Stephanie? She and Stephanie had loved ghost stories. If ghosts existed, Maya was sure Stephanie would have turned into one and come back to visit.

"Have you seen any ghosts yet?" Gwenda asked.

"No," Maya said. She'd seen a fairy. But she wasn't ready to talk about that. "Nothing I'd call a ghost."

"Will you tell us if you see any?" Benjamin asked. "We're interested in all that supernatural stuff."

"So am I. Have *you* ever seen a ghost?"

Benjamin coughed into his hand. People shuffled feet under the table. Nobody answered.

Interesting. They could have just said no.

"Why's it called Spring House?" she asked.

"There was a spring under that spot a long time ago," Kallie said.

"When?"

"Maybe a hundred years ago."

"Huh." Maya frowned. "Hey. What are you eating?"

"Special food," Benjamin said. "Our family has a special diet. This is stew, and pudding, and softbread. Apples. You've seen apples before."

"Sure," she said. The stew steamed and looked brown and green with dark things floating in it. The pudding was caramel colored, and the softbread looked like cornbread pudding— it filled the silver cups like a liquid. The apple was green. She glanced down the table and saw that everybody was eating the same meal. "Is your apartment house a commune?"

"What does that mean?" asked Kallie.

"Like, you guys all know everybody in all the apartments, and maybe you all cook in the same kitchen? Or—" If they had strict rules about food, maybe they were religious. A cult, even? Maybe she shouldn't be so nosy.

"Of course we know everybody in the building," Benjamin said. "We're all related. And we do have one big kitchen, though every apartment has its own kitchen. My mom makes the school lunches for everybody. It's easier that way."

"Those dishes are really nice." Their food smelled good, too.

Maya opened her paper sack to see what Dad had packed in her lunch. Carrots and celery, PBJ, juice box, a small, red apple, Twinkies, a couple of napkins. The usual. She opened the ziplock bag that held her sandwich and poked the straw into the juice box.

"What is that?" Benjamin asked, peeking at the juice box.

"Apple juice," she said. She glanced around the cafeteria. Other kids had juice boxes.

"I've seen them before, just never up close."

So he probably didn't go grocery shopping with whoever shopped at his house. She shrugged and handed him the box. "You want to taste it?"

His eyebrows rose. Okay, was that too weird a question?

He shook his head and handed the box back. "Thanks, but we're on a special diet," he said again.

"You don't eat store-bought food?"

"Not very often."

"Well," she said and bit into her sandwich.

Nobody talked.

Was she the one killing their fun?

Rowan finished first, repacked his dishes into his tin, pushed away from the table, and stomped off.

Twyla and Gwenda heaved simultaneous sighs. Then they smiled.

Kallie laughed. "Okay, my brother is a big wet cloud," she said.

Maya set down the remains of her sandwich. "Is it just me he hates, or does he hate everybody?"

"Everybody," said Kallie. She frowned. "Well, it's not that he hates them. It's just that people don't behave."

"They don't behave the way he thinks they should, anyway," Gwenda said.

"That's it," Kallie said. "He only wants to run the world."

"He should find the right world and go there and leave us alone." Gwenda scraped the bottom of her bowl, then stuffed a cloth napkin into it. "I wish he'd stop trying to rule me."

"And me," Twyla agreed.

"And me," said Kallie.

They all looked at Benjamin, who shrugged. "He's bossy, but he knows what he's talking about most of the time."

"You're such a *drook*," Kallie said.

"*Drook*?" Maya repeated.

Kallie sighed. "Kind of like a ball of lint or a dust bunny. Fuzzy and without a spine."

"What's *chikuvny*?"

"*Chikuvny?*" Twyla's eyes widened.

Benjamin jumped in before she could say anything else. "I already told you. It's kind of like a perfume."

"In what language? Another guy said it to me this morning. Twice in one morning, a word I never heard before in my life. And I don't wear perfume."

They all stared at her.

"Who said it?" Benjamin asked.

"I don't know. Some guy I bumped into in the hall when I was trying to follow you this morning."

"Nobody at this table?"

"Of course not. It was some guy. Taller than us. I think he's an eighth grader, maybe even a ninth grader. He looked really sick." She took out her notebook and sketched the guy's face. Thin face, strong jawline. Wavy hair. Shadows under the eyes, the cheeks almost hollow. Narrow lips, a long nose, freckles. "He said, 'Where's the portal?'" She turned the notebook around and showed them the sketch. "The portal. Like, huh?" She shrugged.

They all stared at it, paying much more attention than people usually did.

"Gwenda?" Benjamin said.

Gwenda shook her head, her fingers playing with the

patterned stone charms on her bracelet. "No one I've ever seen."

"He didn't tell you his name?" Benjamin asked Maya.

"We didn't have much of a conversation. I asked him where M44 was, and he didn't know. Why? Why are you guys acting weird? What's so important about perfume?" Perfume she wasn't even wearing.

She glanced at her hand. The faint dusting of gold caught her eye.

Wait. She *was* wearing it.

Fairy dust. These people could smell fairy dust. They had a name for it.

And so did the stranger she had bumped into before class.

* SEVEN *

"It's just not that common a scent," Benjamin said. "We figure anybody who knows where to get it must . . ."

She held her hand up to her face, sniffed her fingers. The spicy scent had faded. She reached out and, finally, touched the skin on the back of Benjamin's hand. Faint tingles, not like the sizzles she'd felt when she grabbed the stranger's arm that morning.

He twitched his fingers a couple of times. She lifted her hand away.

She was losing it, her evidence that the fairy had been in her room.

All these people knew something about it, though. Even though they wouldn't talk, they knew something.

"Where do you buy *chikuvny*?" she asked.

Benjamin and Gwenda exchanged glances. Gwenda turned to her. "Actually, it's a controlled substance."

"You mean it's like drugs? Jeez!"

"Not so much drugs . . ." Benjamin said. "Maybe more like diamonds? Or uranium?"

Maya frowned, trying to follow.

"Maya, can we have that picture?" Twyla asked.

"Sure." She ripped her picture of Sick Boy out of her notebook.

"Thanks." Twyla bit her lip. "Someone should take this home," she said. She glanced at the others, who nodded, but nobody took the sketch. "I guess I'll do it."

"Whoa, this *is* important?" Maya asked.

"It might be. We can't tell you why, though," said Benjamin.

"Arrrrgh!" She could already tell they would be frustrating friends.

Frustrating, but fascinating.

Sooner or later she'd get them to talk.

The bell rang, signaling the end of lunch. She shoved her apple and Twinkies into her backpack for later.

"Ready for *español*?" Benjamin asked. "Señora Hernandez?"

She dragged her schedule out of her pocket. "Oh, yeah! I always wanted to learn another language. What language do you guys speak?"

"Kerlinqua," said Gwenda. "Kind of a family language—not a lot of places in the world where you can speak it."

"Spanish is much more useful," Benjamin said.

"We can show you the way to class," said Gwenda. "Benjamin and I are both taking it."

They said good-bye to Kallie and Twyla and hit the halls.

Kids moved away from them. There was room around them, even though the corridor was crowded.

"You guys are wearing an antiperfume, right?" Maya asked. "What do you call that? *Nyvukchi*?"

Gwenda smiled, and Benjamin shook his head and smiled a little, too. "It's not the way we smell," he said.

"We've all known each other since kindergarten, and the older kids in our families knew each other before we got here. This has been going on for more than a hundred years," said Gwenda. She stopped, gripped Maya's shoulder as Benjamin slipped past them into the room.

Maya looked up. They were at the doorway to their Spanish class.

Gwenda pulled Maya to the side. "You chose us, and we're

social suicide. You can stick with us now, and there you'll be, out of the mainstream, pretty much," she said in a quiet voice. "Or ditch us now and make regular friends. We won't be upset."

"But we're neighbors."

"So what? You've got lots of other neighbors. You'll make other friends."

Maya shook her head. "I like you guys."

"I like you, too," Gwenda told her, "but we, well, we don't make the best friends. Really. We can't invite you home. We have lots of after-school activities, extra studies, that take up almost all our spare time, and we don't eat normal food or watch TV."

"Are you guys in some kind of religious cult?"

Gwenda looked surprised, then nodded. "I guess you could call it that."

"I could invite you to my house, though, right? Or are you not allowed to see how outsiders live?"

"We're allowed to see anything we want," Gwenda said, "if we can find time for it."

Second bell rang. The halls had cleared. Gwenda went past Maya into the classroom.

Maya stood at the head of the class, studying the other

kids. They looked perfectly nice. She might find her next best friend anywhere in this room.

She glanced toward the back row, where Benjamin and Gwenda had staked out their territory, surrounded by empty desks. A glow warmed her from the inside.

Social suicide or mainstream?

She headed for the back of the classroom and sat down next to Gwenda.

Maya had never taken a foreign language before, so Spanish class surprised her in a lot of ways. She knew a few words of Danish because her grandparents spoke it, and she'd learned one or two things in French, because she had lived in northern Idaho—close to the Canadian border, a lot of the labels on food were bilingual and the names of towns were French, though they weren't pronounced the way a French person would pronounce them.

She was still mulling over Spanish vocabulary words when Benjamin nudged her arm in the hallway. "I'll show you the way to art class," he said, and she smiled. She'd been looking forward to art all day.

There were no desks in the art room, just big, paint-splattered, scratched-up tables with chairs around them. Benjamin and Maya sat at the table farthest back.

Every other table filled up. More people she recognized from their essays in language arts: Movie Extra Jessie, Multiple Movie Girl Keisha, Tovah, whom Gwenda had run off to compare summers with before school—What was up with that? If the Janus House kids didn't have any outside friends, how come Gwenda and Tovah seemed so tight?— Guitar Hero Alex, and Campout Boy Steve, they were all in art class.

Travis strolled in right before second bell. "Hey," he said. He dropped into the chair next to Maya's and slumped immediately.

"Hey," Maya said, and smiled at him. She was relieved that he didn't seem to hate her after the dumb stuff she had said at lunch. She wondered if he would fall asleep again.

A black woman with really short hair and a red-and-orange tunic and trousers came in and set a bunch of giant pieces of paper on the teacher's raised desk at the front of the room. She wrote MS. JAMILA on the green board, then turned and beamed at them.

"Hi. I'm Ms. Jamila," she said. "Welcome to art!"

Maya grinned. She settled in her chair. For the first time all day she felt completely comfortable.

After she took attendance, Ms. Jamila said, "Now I want you to forget everything you know about art and start new!"

The one thing Maya could do well, and she was supposed to forget it?

Ms. Jamila walked from table to table, handing each student a giant piece of paper. "Spread out as much as possible," she said. "You three have plenty of room, don't you?" She smiled at Benjamin, Maya, and Travis. "Each take a side of the table. Here."

Ms. Jamila returned to the front of the class and got a shoe box, then walked around the room again. "Take three colors each," she said. Kids pulled big fat marking pens out of the shoe box.

By the time the teacher got to them, there weren't many choices left. Travis snagged a green pen and Benjamin got a red. They also got brown and gray. Maya got brown, gray, and black.

"Okay, class! Let's do something wild! I want you to draw a picture of your family. But not a portrait! More a picture of who they are inside. If you're right-handed, I want you to draw this with your left hand. If you're left-handed, draw it with your right hand. No cheating! This isn't about making a picture that looks good, it's about finding out something you didn't know you knew."

Movie Extra Jessie raised her hand.

"Yes?"

"Can we share markers? Three colors isn't very many."

"I know. It's part of the challenge. I want you to work with what you have. Sometimes limits teach us how to expand inside them."

"What does *that* mean?" Travis mumbled to Maya.

Maya shrugged. She was already mad that she was supposed to draw with her left hand. Sometimes she had contests with her sister Candra to see who could write the neatest with her left hand. Neither of them was good at it. She hated that the first picture she did in this class was going to be a bad one.

Well, she could draw the assignment really fast and then get back to her sketchbook.

"Ready? Begin!" said Ms. Jamila. Kids bent heads over their tables. Markers squeaked.

Maya started with black. Okay, a symbol for each member of her family.

Candra was easy: a camera, with a big long lens that stared out of the picture like a giant eyeball.

Peter was—well, Peter should be some kind of animal, Maya guessed. There wasn't an animal alive he didn't want to catch or touch or study. Which was his favorite? Maybe a dog, though his favorite changed all the time. She drew a picture of Sully to stand for Peter.

What was she going to put when she drew Sully, though? A food bowl. She drew one with Sully's name on it. She drew chunks of meat inside. Not that you could tell. She shaded them with brown and gray, and that helped a little bit.

What could she draw for Mom and Dad? They were both teachers, but was that who they were inside? Maya thought about teacher symbols. Apples. Books. Chalkboard. Erasers? Erasers might be nice. Get rid of everything you didn't like. But that didn't really define either of her parents.

For Mom she drew a piano. Every Saturday night in Idaho, they had had a jam session in the living room after supper. Mom played the piano and gave Maya and Candra turns—she'd offered everybody in the family piano lessons, but Candra and Maya practiced, and Peter didn't. Dad played an acoustic guitar he'd had for a million years, Peter kept time on some old bongos or sometimes played wooden spoons, and everybody sang—sometimes new songs, sometimes ones they'd known for years.

Maya loved the way Music Night used to be. Her friends from school always wanted to come over Saturday nights to join them, and Mom's and Dad's friends came too. People brought other instruments: mandolins, fiddles, banjos, harmonicas, accordions, even a string bass once in a while.

Stephanie had always come. She couldn't play an instrument, but she had loved to sing.

Sometimes it got too crowded in their old living room, but that made it more fun. In summer, Music Night spilled out onto the porch.

In Oregon, so far, Candra wanted to ditch Music Night. She thought Music Night was dorky. The songs they played were too old and corny. Even though the Andersens had a much bigger living room now, they hadn't had a Music Night in the new house yet.

Maybe Music Night was another thing they lost in the move, like Maya's doll and Peter's snakeskin collection.

Maya decided to draw a book to stand for her father. Sunday night was Read-Aloud Night. Dad had started it before Maya was born. He read from a book to them every Sunday night. When Maya first learned to read, she couldn't wait a whole week to find out what happened next in *The Hobbit*, so she sneaked a look. When Dad read the part out loud that she had already read to herself, it lost a lot of shine. She had never looked ahead again.

Maya drew Dad's book with the front edge showing, and behind it she put a shadow of Dad's shape. She sketched in Mom's piano, drew outlines of two hands across it, and colored in the piano around the hands. Sully cast a Peter-shaped shadow on the ground. Behind Candra's camera she shaded in an outline of her sister, too.

Finally she put herself in the picture. A paintbrush, standing on end, one of those fat-tipped sable ones. She wished she had a color she could put on the tip of the brush, red or blue or green. Behind the brush she outlined the shadow of a girl.

She sat back, chewed her lip, looked at her picture. Should she put more in? Candra's great telephone voice, and how she could ask questions so people always told her more than they meant to? Peter's weird occasional psychic flashes and strange friendships? She had come outside one morning and found him sitting on the ground, feeding crumbs to birds. They were eating out of his hand. Wild birds. As soon as they noticed her, they flew away.

She looked at her picture and saw that it was balanced. Dark places and light places, the camera and the paintbrush between the book and the piano and slightly lower, then down in front Sully/Peter, sitting there looking up with his tongue lolling out in a dog smile, his boy shadow stretching off to the left and the dog dish representing Sully on the right.

Maya added some brown and gray shadows where they would do some good and then stopped. Good enough. She was done.

She capped her markers and sat back, smiling.

Ms. Jamila was standing behind her. She leaned forward, startling Maya. "This is very good," she murmured, "but which hand do you usually draw with?"

Maya looked at her hands.

She had drawn the whole picture with her right hand, and she had random ink marks on her fingers to prove it.

She had messed up her first assignment.

"It's okay," Ms. Jamila said. She patted Maya's shoulder. "I know the impulse is strong." She went up and got another piece of paper. "Try something different this time, with your left hand, okay? Draw a picture of a garden you've never seen."

Maya licked her lip. She nodded. She held her black marker in her left hand and started drawing.

Stupid left hand, so clumsy. Better make this simple. She drew black branches with black thorns on them, more and more, and when she had a big thicket of leafless sticker bushes, she drew a lacy black iron fence around the outside, all jagged because her left hand didn't want to cooperate. She made its resistance part of the picture.

Yeah.

She finished by drawing one gray flower, its center shaped like a face, on top of a bush.

Then she checked out Benjamin's picture.

Whoa.

Maya didn't know what he had drawn, but there were lots of them. Swirls and loops, little tornadoes or hurricanes, but all of them had a clear spot in the middle, with loops all around, as if light glared from the center of every storm.

"Gosh," Maya said, "how can you tell who's who?" There must have been fifty of those gray, red, and brown things on the page.

"It doesn't matter," said Benjamin. "We're more alike than we are different."

That shocked her. She and Candra were always looking for ways to be different from each other, and Peter was totally different, too.

"Which one is you?" Maya asked.

Benjamin's eyebrows rose. He scanned his page of storms

and finally pointed to a small one near the bottom. It was gray and brown, with not much red in it.

"Huh," she said.

Travis looked, too. He frowned. "Hey, Maya, let's see yours."

Ms. Jamila said, "All right, class, time's about up! Five more minutes to finish what you've started, and then we'll look at what we've produced."

Maya slid her family picture out from under the sticker-garden picture and showed it to Travis and Benjamin.

"Wow," said Travis.

"Ditto," said Benjamin in a soft voice. "You're the brush?"

"Yeah."

"It's very cool," said Travis.

"Thanks." Maya set the picture down again, feeling awkward. "You show me yours?"

He held his up.

She couldn't tell what he had drawn. Three messes side by side was what it looked like. Lots of green and brown and gray loops, some awkward blobs stacked on top of each other. It looked like a left-handed picture, all right. Everything jerky and sprawling over the lines.

"Uh," Maya said. She couldn't think of a single complimentary thing to say, but she didn't want to hurt his feelings.

"See? This is me." Travis pointed to the mess on the right. "This is my dad." The mess in the middle. "And this is Oma, my grandma." The mess on the left. "Teacher said draw what we look like inside, so this is the guts, and here's the stomach, and these spongy things are lungs, and I had to make the hearts green, and this gray thing on top is the brain, and—"

Maya threw a pen at him. It hit him in the chest. He tumbled back off his chair. "You wound me!" he said from the floor, where he had fallen artistically into a sprawl.

"Hey! Settle down back there!" Ms. Jamila came back to their table and said, "What's the problem?"

Oh, no! What if she got detention her first day in school? In *art* class?

"Artistic differences," Benjamin said.

Travis lurched to his feet. "Sorry. I was fooling around, teacher," he said.

"It's my fault. I threw a pen at him." Maya couldn't get Travis in trouble when it was really her fault. He had a reputation to live down already.

"Artistic differences?" Ms. Jamila asked Benjamin.

Benjamin pointed to Travis's picture. "What he and his

father and grandmother look like inside," Benjamin said.

Ms. Jamila studied Travis's picture, then laughed. "I understand," she said after she managed to stop. "Maya, in my class, everybody gets the freedom to express themselves however they choose. We don't criticize unless the artist asks for feedback. Everybody can praise anybody else's work, though." Her voice had risen to reach the whole room, and the other kids were listening. "Travis, why don't you take your picture up front and show it to us? Everyone, remember. You can say good things about each other's projects or say nothing at all; those are your options. Let's go."

One by one everybody took their pictures up front to show, and Maya got more insight into who she was going to school with.

Ms. Jamila called Maya up last.

Maya went up front. "I did the assignment wrong," she said. "I forgot to draw with my left hand." She held up her picture. She knew it was good. She felt blood burning in her cheeks.

Some people said *ahh*! One or two gasped.

"Wow," said Guitar Hero Alex, "you draw like in comic books."

"Thanks," she said. "It's my favorite thing. I've been prac-

ticing for years. That's why this paintbrush is me." She explained the rest of her family, and then the bell rang.

It was going to be okay. She was pretty sure.

Art was the last class of the day. Afterward, Travis walked her
to the counselor's office so she could pick up some forms and
a school map. "I come here all the time," he said.

"I don't get that about you," she said. "Why did you
flunk?"

He shrugged and looked away. "It's complicated. Later,
dudette."

"Okay. Thanks for your help."

He shrugged again as he headed down the hall toward
the front door, weaving between other homeward-headed
students.

The corridors were empty when she left Mrs. Boleslav's
office. She wondered if she could find her locker on her own
now that she had a map. If she went straight home, she'd
just have to sit around and do homework, so why not ex-
plore?

She dug out the map and the piece of paper with her
locker assignment on it. Corridor G, locker bank 2, #1512.

Corridor G. Sure. She scanned the walls to see if the corridors were labeled. Not as far as she could see.

She checked the first locker bank she came to. Numbers ran from 500 to 600. Which corridor was she in? Was corridor G even in the main building?

She walked down the hall and checked out another bank of lockers: 2700 to 2800. Sha, very helpful.

This was dumb. She could just ask Travis tomorrow. She turned to head for the exit and found herself face to face with the tall, freckled boy from that morning.

He looked even sicker than he had before. He stared at her, his nostrils flaring.

Then he grabbed her arm and dragged her into the nearest classroom.

* EIGHT *

"What? What do you want?" she asked. They were in a science classroom. Sharp chemical smells. Lab tables, stools, Bunsen burners, test tubes. The squeak of mice running on wheels.

"I need your help."

She tried to twist out of his grasp, but he was stronger than he looked. "Let go. What's the matter with you? This isn't funny."

"No. Not funny. Please stand still."

Fear pumped through her, prickled against the back of her neck, loosened her knees. She was alone in the middle of an empty school with some crazy, strong boy.

"What do you want?" She tugged at her arm, tried to push him away. She couldn't budge him.

Should she scratch him? Her fingernails weren't very long. Maybe she should bite him. Or kick him. Dad had told her where to kick guys if they were threatening her.

"Let go," she said again. She didn't want to wait until it was too late to kick him if she had to, to protect herself. But she didn't want to kick him if there was an easier way to get away.

He heaved a sigh. His breath smelled like he'd been throwing up. Air rasped in and out of him. His freckles stood out starkly against his milk-pale skin. He was sick and sweaty and still way stronger than she was.

"Please," he said.

He let go of her and thumped down on a stool, covered his face with his hands. "Please," he whispered.

She edged away and put a lab table between them. She wouldn't let him catch her again. Her wrist was already bruised where he'd gripped it. Should she run?

Chikuvny.

A controlled substance? Fairy dust? Something he knew about. Maybe he'd tell her more than Benjamin or Gwenda had.

"What do you want?" she asked for the third time.

"I need help. I need help of someone who comes from

this Earth, someone knows where a portal is. Please. It's not for me. Won't you please help me?" His voice was full of despair.

"It depends on what you want me to do."

He plunged his hand into his pocket. "Look," he whispered.

In his cupped hand was something that looked like a small egg, only instead of a shell, it was covered in a thin, velvety skin. It glowed from inside, soft pastel colors, pink, green, yellow, blue, occasional streaks of silvery light. Some of it looked dark and sick, though.

She edged closer and leaned in to look. So beautiful. So damaged. She swallowed a rising sadness.

"Do you know this? Do you know this *sissimi*? How it is?" He had some kind of accent. She hadn't noticed it before, and now that she did, she couldn't figure out what kind it was, only that it was getting thicker. "That it's a treasure, a precious," he whispered. "A bond? A seer?"

"I don't know."

"Your hand." He took her hand, lifted it to his nose, and sniffed. "But is fading," he said, his voice heavy. "But so am I."

"I don't know what a *sissimi* is. I don't know anything about a portal. I don't know what *chikuvny* is."

"You don't know! You don't know." His dark blue eyes looked sad. He lowered his eyelids, then glanced up at her again. "I am sorry. I found the wrong person. I have been searching for days. I could not find any of the right people. But look. She is dying."

They stared at the egg. As Maya watched, another patch of it dimmed.

"I am not from here. I don't have the right—" He frowned. He pinched the skin of his arm. "The right. So I can't give the *sissimi* what she needs. You could do that."

"What? You want me to feed it?"

"Yes."

"How?"

"You could save her. You could keep her alive long enough to find a portal, and then she could get home. At her home they will know what to do. You understand?"

"No."

"No," he repeated. His shoulders sagged. "I stole her. The Krithi told me how. They said she would be my perfect friend. They told me what *sissimi* grow into. Companions. Collectors. Protectors. The Krithi said I could raise her here, far from her home. Then none of her masters can find me. I didn't know she needs local host, or she doesn't get the right—" He made a growling sound and shook his head. "Food, nutriment. I didn't know," he whispered.

Maya bit her lower lip.

"You can save her."

"How?"

"Feed her. Keep her careful. She will hatch soon if she survives. Then she will be your companion. Your seer."

She touched the egg. Light flared around her fingertip. The velvet skin turned damp. Her fingertip burned and tingled.

She snatched her hand back.

"Please," he said again. "I should not have stolen her. I am killing her. She is rare. She is precious. Please save her."

"What do I have to do?"

"Just feed her. She will do the rest."

"Feed her what?"

"Well, it is something inside you. She needs it. She needs the local. But she won't hurt you."

"What are you talking about?"

"She will die," he whispered. "Please."

Why was she even listening to this nut job? She should back away right now. He didn't look like he was strong enough to chase her anymore.

Last night she saw a fairy. Maybe this guy wasn't crazy. Anything could happen.

She should call 911 and get him an ambulance.

The egg sparkled, and then half of it dimmed.

She gasped. It shouldn't die, no matter what it was, not if there was something she could do to stop it. "What do I have to do?"

"Say yes."

"Yes, okay, yeah. What does it eat? Cereal?"

He gripped her left hand and pressed the egg against the inside of her wrist. The egg felt warm, then hot and wet, then prickling, then pricking, definitely pricking.

"Oww!" she yelled. Pain shot up her arm. She jerked, tried to get away from the boy, but he held her hand tight.

It hurt, oh, it hurt. It felt like a vacuum sucking her skin, then her blood, muscles, bones. Were her fingers turning to dust? Did the egg suck them dry? She wouldn't even have a hand in a minute. She felt her arm shrinking and shriveling. Hot needles pricked their way up her arm, into her shoulder.

Stupid, stupid—why hadn't she run when she could?

She cried and sobbed and jerked against the boy's hold, but he didn't let her go. "It will be all right," he said. "She won't hurt you."

What did he think it was doing now? She had never felt

such horrible, shocking, burning pain! Tears streamed down her face.

Her left arm went numb.

Better.

In a way.

She reached over with her right hand and tried to push the egg off her wrist. But it wasn't loose anymore. It had sunk into her flesh, slipped under her skin, leaving only a glowing bump at her wrist. She couldn't pry it off.

The boy caught her other hand before she could start digging with her fingernails.

"No," he whispered. "Don't kill her. You have saved her. Don't undo it all now." He pressed a few places on her shoulder, and suddenly her right arm went dead. It hung by her side. She couldn't lift it.

"Please," he said. "She won't hurt you. She will only be with you. She will only love you."

"It hurt! It was the worst pain I ever felt! It hurt."

"I'm sorry." His eyes were wet. "Yes. I forgot. At first it hurts, but not for long. By tomorrow you'll be fine. And she will survive." He let go of her left hand. "Thank you. Thank you ultimately and endlessly. You will have to teach her. She won't know right away."

"Teach her what?" Her left arm was numb. She had felt

it being sucked dry. She thought about lifting her arm, and to her surprise, it rose. And it looked normal, except for the glowing bump. She turned her hand, looked at its top, then its bottom. Normal, not shriveled up into a dried-out sack of skin.

The bump on her wrist glowed with colored radiance. Lights moved under the skin of her left forearm and flowed up to her elbow, then farther up her arm, as though fireflies swam in her veins.

"Teach her?" she cried. "How can I teach something that's eating me from the inside out? What did you do to me? Make it stop!"

"I can't. She won't eat you. She only needs you very much. She is made to work with people, all kinds of people. You will be fine." He lifted her hands and kissed the palm of each of them. "I am sorry I frightened you," he murmured. He lumbered to his feet and staggered out of the room.

She followed him out into the hall. She had to get home. She had to tell Mom and Dad what had happened and make them take her to a doctor.

The corridor to the entrance stretched for miles. Light from outside came from the far end of a long, dim tunnel. The boy was nowhere in sight. Her head felt light and floaty, and she could barely lift her feet off the ground.

She shuffled. One foot forward, then the next.

Shuffle, shuffle, shuffle, her arms swinging by her sides, beyond her control.

After a while, she stopped and leaned against some lockers. The glimmer of light at the entrance looked almost as far away as it had before.

The egg was dying, but it was killing her first, and she didn't think it was a fair trade. On the other hand, she felt so tired and sick and faint she almost didn't care.

She started to slip down the wall to the floor.

No!

She shuffled forward before she could fall down. If she could make it outside, someone would see her.

Where was everybody? How long had she been shut up in the science room with that crazy guy?

"Help," she yelled as she shuffled toward the exit, but it came out as a tiny muffled squeak. Maybe if she had headed back toward Mrs. Boleslav's office instead of toward the doors, she could have reached it by now. Even if Mrs. Boleslav was gone, there were phones there.

Cell phone. Dad had gotten everyone a cell phone when they arrived in Oregon. "Since we're all going to different places now, we need a way to check in. These are just for calling the family. Don't go texting your friends all day," he had said when he handed them out, but he smiled when he said it.

Maya had thought, *Friends? What friends?* She had settled down and learned how to use her phone, like everybody else in the family. No camera on the phone, no music player, nothing fancy. Just a calling device.

Which she could sure use now.

Her cell phone was in her right pocket. She tried to reach across with her left hand. She couldn't wriggle her left hand down into the pocket. Her right hand was dead.

She couldn't muster the energy to look back and see if the office was any closer than the entrance.

Why wasn't the janitor cruising the corridors and making sure everybody was gone?

She kept shuffling. Gradually the entrance doors got nearer.

"Help," she muttered. She leaned forward, then got her feet under her before she could fall. Leaned forward, shuffled her feet forward. Leaned forward . . .

She just wanted to lie down. Maybe sleep for twenty-four hours.

What if she woke up dead?

Keep moving.

Her stomach gurgled, then growled.

She was starving.

Keep moving.

Next thing she knew, she had her forehead pressed against cool glass, and it sure felt good.

The glass moved and she fell forward. Someone caught her before she fell flat on her face.

"Maya?"

"Travis," she said, in her tiny squeaky voice.

"Maya! What happened to you?" He gripped her shoulders.

"Help," she said.

"Help? Help!" He looked back over his shoulder frantically. "Hey, you sit here and I'll go get somebody." He started to lower her to the ground.

She clutched his arm with her left hand. "Home," she said. "Three blocks."

"What? You should go to the hospital! What happened? Did somebody hit you?"

She closed her eyes. Dizziness made her sway. Travis could call for help on her phone, if he didn't have one of his own. What kind of help did she want? Mom? Dad? A hospital? The pain in her left wrist had eased. Right now, her pain centered in her stomach. She said, "No. Nobody hit me. I've got to get home. I—I'm starving!"

"What?" He slipped her backpack off her back and slid his arms through the straps, then leaned over and put his arm around her.

It occurred to her that if she weren't so brain-dead and worried, this might be an interesting situation.

It occurred to her that she must feel a little better than she had, or things wouldn't occur to her.

Her stomach rumbled like an earthquake. She felt sick with hunger, headachy with it.

"Which way?" he asked.

She pointed to the right. "Thirty-third Street," she muttered.

Travis dragged her toward home.

✷ NINE ✷

He was so great about it. He practically carried her for three blocks. She could barely put one foot in front of the other.

As they lurched past Janus House, Benjamin ran outside. "What happened?" he asked.

"I don't know," Travis said. "She came out of school and fell over."

Benjamin rushed to her left side. He reached for her hand.

When he touched her, a spark flew out.

"Ack!" He jerked back. "What?" He gingerly reached out to her left hand, and it shocked him again. She turned her hand over and showed him the glowing lump under her skin. "Maya!" he cried. *"Kiri alamaka!"*

"Jeez! What *is* that thing?" said Travis.

"I don't know," she wailed. "Chikuvny Boy put it there."

Benjamin sucked air in between his teeth, a hissing sound.

"What does *that* mean?" Travis asked her.

"It means she needs to come to my house," Benjamin said. "It's closer." He leaned over and talked to her left wrist. "I won't hurt you," he murmured. "Let me help you."

He touched her hand, and this time it didn't shock him. He and Travis pulled her up the path, up the porch steps, across the porch, and through the front doors of Janus House.

In the carpeted foyer there was a broad stairway in front of them, a door to the right and a door to the left, and other doors farther down the hall past the staircase. Benjamin nodded toward the left-hand door.

"I'm so hungry," Maya moaned.

The door opened into a dark room. It smelled like incense and spice. Thick patterned rugs lay on the floor. Dark cloth sprinkled with tiny mirrors covered the walls and ceiling, draped and billowy. It was like walking into some kind of tent. At night.

"That way," Benjamin said, nodding toward an arched doorway.

The smell of fresh baking made her mouth water. They went through the arch into a kitchen, which was much lighter than the living room.

Benjamin and Travis lowered her into a wooden chair. Then Benjamin went to the counter by the stove and returned with a big loaf of brown-crusted pound cake.

It smelled heavenly. Her right hand shot out and grabbed a handful. The cake came away in a moist hunk. Inside the crust, it was lemon yellow.

She stuffed it into her mouth. It tasted as good as anything she'd ever eaten. She swallowed it without chewing and grabbed more.

Benjamin set a glass of water in front of her. "Eat as much as you want," he said. "I'll go get help. Stay here."

Pound cake! Could anything be better? She ate half the loaf, so happy she was almost crying.

Then she glanced at Travis, who sat nearby.

He stared at her as if she had turned into a wolf girl.

"Sorry," she said. "Usually I have better manners. I'm so hungry I can't stop myself."

"It's all right," he murmured. But he shook his head

while he said it, like he meant it was all wrong.

So maybe she should have used a knife, cut off slices before she ate them. But she didn't have a knife.

"Do you want some?" she asked.

"No. Nope. I'm fine. You eat."

Her stomach still flamed with hunger, but she slowed down. Travis had rescued her. He had already proved he was a good friend. She didn't want him to think she was a total dork.

She glanced around the kitchen now that the first edge was off her hunger. The walls were yellow, except one covered with a huge tapestry so faded she couldn't tell what the picture on it was supposed to be. The table she sat at was carved wooden lace, inlaid with ivory or bone. A brass chandelier hung above it, spangled with lots of little lightbulbs.

She reached for the glass of water.

With her right hand.

Wait a sec, she'd grabbed the cake with her right hand, too. She could use her arm again. Thank God. She shook her right arm, rotated her hand. After Chikuvny Boy used that Vulcan arm pinch on her, she had been afraid maybe she'd never be able to move her arm again.

She lifted her left arm. It worked when she thought orders at it, but she couldn't sense it very well yet. The strange lump on her wrist still glowed with internal light, colors blooming and fading. Now that she felt better, everything that had just happened seemed even weirder. She cupped her right hand over the lump. It felt velvety soft and warm.

"Explain to me again how that got there," Travis said. "Who's Chickie Boy?"

"Some weird sick kid at school. He said he had this pet, and he needed someone local to take care of it. I said okay, and then he—" She lifted her hand and stared at the lump. Her eyes felt hot. "I didn't know it meant *this*."

"That's a pet? I've seen hairless cats and wiener dogs, and I thought those were ridiculous. But this—"

"You're not helping," Maya said. She swallowed her sadness and ate more cake.

Benjamin came back with Gwenda, who carried a small black lidded cauldron. She looked like a witch.

"I've got some soup for you," Gwenda said. She set the cauldron on the table near Maya and removed the lid. Steam rose, and Maya smelled—heaven. "This is for strength and stamina," Gwenda said. She got a brown clay bowl out of a cupboard and brought it and a ladle to the table. She dished up some soup.

"Here," Benjamin said. He gave Maya a wooden spoon.

If Gwenda was a witch, maybe the soup was a spell. But Maya didn't care. She felt like she'd been waiting to eat this soup for ages. It was just right, not hot enough to burn her tongue, not too cool. It tasted like vinegar and sour grass and spinach. Normally she didn't like any of those things. What was wrong with her?

Vinegar, sour grass, spinach, maybe mushrooms, and something that tasted like pine bark smelled. Suddenly her favorite food in the whole world, even better than pound cake. She could feel it making her strong and well, chasing away all the tired.

"Travis, you want something to drink?" Gwenda asked.

"Yeah, I guess," said Travis. "What you got?"

She went to a turquoise refrigerator and looked inside. "Root beer," she said.

"My favorite."

Gwenda poured a glassful of brown liquid. She moved her fingers over it and handed it to Travis.

He took a sip, then a gulp. "Wow. It's the best I've ever tasted." He lifted the glass to his lips and tilted his head back. Maya, spooning up delicious sour soup, watched Travis set the mostly full glass down and yawn.

His eyes dropped shut. He slumped in his chair.

Maya froze with the spoon in midair. "Did you just drug him?" she asked, panicked.

"Uh-huh. It's for the best. We can't let him find out what happened to you, Maya," Benjamin said.

He sounded like he already knew.

She dropped the spoon and cupped her right hand over her left wrist. She felt a pulse under her palm. Her pulse or the egg's?

If root beer could knock Travis out, what was this soup doing to her?

She sat back and checked in with herself.

She had been faint with hunger and pain when Travis brought her here, had wondered if she was going to die. Now she felt . . . almost normal again. Maybe the soup was just what Gwenda had said. For stamina and strength.

She looked at Gwenda.

"We won't hurt you," Gwenda said gently.

Maya had heard that already today, from Chikuvny Boy, right before Big Pain.

"We won't, Maya. Travis will be fine. He'll wake up in a couple hours without even a headache."

"But—"

"There are some things," Benjamin said, "lots of things, we can't share without good reason."

"This is major, Maya," Gwenda said, "like, change-the-rest-of-your-life big. It's something most people can't help you with, but I think we can. I hope we can." She shook her head. "I don't know. It might even be my fault. I've made so many mistakes lately. Please let us help you."

How could it be Gwenda's fault? She didn't even know Chikuvny Boy.

Chikuvny Boy. Her egg. Change the rest of her life?

The back of her throat felt tight. She uncovered the egg. The glowing, colored bump had collected back the little lights that had been swimming around under the skin of her forearm. It was warm and strange, though she was getting used to it, the way she could no longer bend her wrist all the way. She opened and closed her fingers. They worked fine.

She could go home with this, and then what? She was pretty sure no doctor she could find in the phone book would know what it was or how to treat it.

She sniffled, then nodded. "What is this?" she asked Benjamin. "Do you already know about it?"

"We don't recognize it, but we know about strange," he said. "We deal with strange every day."

Maya's heartbeat sped up. She felt a prickling across her scalp and down the back of her neck. She had an image of herself standing with her hand on a doorknob, about to turn it and open a door into another world.

Benjamin said, "Did Chikuvny Boy tell you why he gave you the—the—"

"*Sissimi*," she said.

"*Sissimi*?" said Benjamin. "Wasn't there something about that in the—"

"*Sissimi*," Gwenda said at the same time. "You have a name for it! That's the first power. I'll be right back." She rose and left, then returned carrying a big, battered, leather-covered book. It was way fatter than the book Benjamin had been reading at school, and it looked even more beat up.

Gwenda and Benjamin sat at the table with Maya and the sleeping Travis. "Did he tell you anything about it?" Benjamin asked Maya.

She touched the bump. It felt velvety-soft and warm. She tried to remember exactly what Chikuvny Boy had told her. "He said it's a treasure and a perfect friend. He said it needs somebody local. He was really sick, and the *sissimi* was dying. I guess he wasn't local enough, though how can that be? The *sissimi* needs to eat me. He didn't tell me that part until after he put it on me, though. I just thought he was going to give it to me and I'd find it some food. Is it some kind of vampire egg?"

"I don't think so," Benjamin said. "There was message traffic—"

"Wait." Gwenda flipped through the book. "*Sissimi*," she said. "Ah. Here you go. They're not parasites. They're protectors. They bond for life. Hmm. It must have been in extreme distress to hook into you like it did. Normally they're helpers, and the connection feels good." She frowned at the book. "Wait a minute. Benjamin? How would you translate *shri*?"

"Stealth?" he said. "Spying?"

She pointed to a passage in the book, and he leaned over to look. Maya looked too. The page was interesting, but there was nothing on it she could read, just strings and swirls of unknown symbols in different colors.

Benjamin frowned at her egg. "'Information feed'?"

"What does *that* mean?" Maya asked.

"There are some words I don't get here, but I think it says *sissimi* are sent out with explorers and spies to gather information and send it back. Send it back to where?" He flipped a page and searched through more explosions of symbols.

Gwenda scanned down the page, moving her fingertip. "Oh, why is this book always so confusing?" she cried at last.

Maya stroked her egg with a fingertip. A silent vibration started in its heart, a purr without noise. It felt lovely, and colors shimmered under her fingertip, shifting from indigo to orange to yellow. "How could this send anything anywhere? Is it like a radio?" she asked.

"The book doesn't explain," said Gwenda. "It never does."

"Does it say how I can get it off?" She pressed the egg to her cheek, felt the thrum against her face and in her arm. Warm. Soothing. Nice. Maybe she didn't want to get it off.

"I don't think it comes off now until it hatches," said Benjamin.

"How long does that take?"

He shook his head. "The book doesn't say. We need more information."

"Listen to this," Gwenda said. "'The *sissimi* bond is so pleasant that unsuitable people seek it out. *Sissimi* nurseries are heavily guarded. Only special people are allowed to bond.'"

"How special am I?" Maya asked.

"Well, you're not somebody they picked," Benjamin said. "But you're special because you saved it from dying."

"There are nurseries for things like this," Maya muttered. "Nurseries. Where?" She stroked the lump. Color rippled in response to her touch. "How come you guys have even heard of this? Is it something everybody knows about but me?"

"No," Benjamin said. "Very few people know. But we do. It's our job to know."

"Where are these *sissimi* nurseries?" Maya asked.

Gwenda bit her lip, ran her finger over a block of symbols in her book. "Not on Earth," she said.

* TEN *

Okay. *Breathe, Maya.* Okay. She could deal with this.

Maybe.

"What is it?" She touched her egg. Warm as a muffin just out of the oven, soft, with a little give to it, but firm underneath—not rock hard, but solid, like an unripe plum. Colors pulsed over its surface, waves of them shining up through the thin pink membrane of her skin: aquamarine, emerald, rose, turquoise, citrine.

"What does it hatch into?" she asked. "What does it look like?"

Gwenda flipped the pages back and forth. "The book doesn't say. There's no picture."

"Is it an animal? Is it a plant? Is it—is it a fairy?" She stroked her finger over the waves of colors. The egg thrummed.

Gwenda searched the book's pages again. "It says it turns into something different with every species it encounters. No specifics."

"Did Chikuvny Boy tell you anything else?" Benjamin asked.

Maya closed her right hand gently around the egg. It radiated warmth and purred against her palm, against the bones of her left wrist. She felt sleepy. Her stomach was full of pound cake and strange, satisfying soup. She could still taste the sour on her tongue, but she liked it. She felt as though she was wrapped in a warm blanket of good health.

What had the boy said to her? "He said she was a seer. I don't know what that is. Companion. Collector. Protector. He said . . . he said I had to teach her."

"Teach her what?" asked Benjamin.

Maya shook her head. "I don't know."

"Teach her how to be local," Gwenda said slowly. "That's why Chikuvny Boy picked Maya."

"That, and I was wearing *chikuvny*," she said.

They both stared at her.

"He said I could take care of her until she was big enough,

then take her to a portal," she said. "Portals are connected to *chikuvny*, right?"

They didn't answer.

"And you guys know where the portals are. All this time, Chikuvny Boy was looking for you guys. I smelled right; that's why he found me. I smelled like fairy dust. But the fairy came from your house, right?"

Neither of them said anything.

"You saw my drawing. You know I've seen her, Benjamin."

"Yes," he finally admitted.

She knew it. "She got out because Gwenda left the door open?"

Gwenda sighed. "Dumb Rowan. Talking about our business on the street. Next time he tries to get me in trouble, I'm going to use that one."

"You left the door open," Maya said slowly to Gwenda. "The portal?"

"No, not that door," said Benjamin.

"Chikuvny Boy said I had to find a portal," she said, "that she'll need it. She can go home and they'll—whoever they are, wherever they are—they'll know what to do. Is that right?"

"We really can't talk about this. Not without permission." Benjamin's face was blank.

"You can't even tell me whether the fairy is safe? She slept on me last night."

"That's wild," Gwenda said. "She was very skittery. She had never used a portal before, and it totally spooked her. But yeah, she moved on okay."

"Gwenda!" Benjamin cried.

"She needs to know, Benjamin, you know she does." Gwenda turned to her. "We're not supposed to talk to *anybody*. So we don't make friends with other kids. We don't talk to strangers. We spend all our time together. Like a religious cult."

"But you let me sit with you."

Benjamin said, "You smelled right. We thought maybe you were family from out of town. Although even the youngest of us knows to get rid of that scent before leaving the house."

She touched her egg to her cheek. It purred silently, comforting her.

All day long, people had mistaken her for something she wasn't. Fairy dust and mistaken identity.

"I told you right away I didn't know what *chikuvny* was," she said to Benjamin.

"You're supposed to pretend you don't know. I should

never have said that word to you. Even if you understood it, you would be right to pretend you didn't."

She shook her head. "That's crazy!"

He smiled. "Yeah."

"We can't keep pretending we don't know, any of us." Gwenda closed the book, put her hands on top of it, and rested her chin on her hands. "Maya has a real problem, and it might relate to our other problems. We have to tell the Elders. We need help."

The front door opened in the other room. Someone called, "Benjamin? Are you home? Why aren't you at energy class? Have you seen Gwenda?"

Rowan walked into the kitchen.

Maya's heart pounded, and she had a hard time catching her breath.

Rowan brushed the hair out of his face and glared at her.

* ELEVEN *

"What's going on here?" Rowan asked in a voice so cold Maya's skin prickled.

Benjamin straightened. "We have a situation."

"Obviously."

Gwenda touched Maya's right hand. "Maya, show him," she said.

Maya hugged the egg to her chest.

"Once begun, must go on," Gwenda said. "Maya, show him."

Maya felt strangely tender about her egg. It purred and comforted her, and it was so beautiful, all soft colored lights. It felt warm against her wrist, against her cheek. What if Rowan wanted to hurt it?

Gwenda had said there was no way to break the bond

between them. Like it or not, her egg was on her to stay until it hatched.

She lowered her wrist and showed it to Rowan.

"What!" he gasped. He came to her and leaned over the egg, then stared at Gwenda.

"It's called a *sissimi*."

"*Sissimi*?" said Rowan. "The alert messages—!" His eyes narrowed.

"Here's the entry," Gwenda said, and handed him the book open to the right page.

He read it, frowning the whole time. Then he gave Maya a glare. "How did this happen?"

"We better explain it to everyone at once," Benjamin said.

Maya had seen a lot of different people come and go from Janus House. Did she have to talk to all of them? "Who's 'everyone'?" she asked.

"Really, just the Elders. Rowan can find out when they do," said Benjamin.

Rowan walked to a picture on the wall and touched a painted cat. The eyes glowed. "This is Rowan. There's been a development. We need an emergency meeting with the Elders," Rowan told the cat.

"Five minutes, in the solar room," the cat said. Or something said it from the picture. The voice was midrange and could have belonged to a man or a woman. The cat's eyes stopped glowing. Rowan dropped his hand from the painting. "How long is Travis out for?" he asked.

"At least another hour," said Gwenda. "Probably an hour and a half."

"Let's go." He turned, then paused in the doorway to the living room, a frown furrowing his forehead.

Gwenda grabbed the battered book and took Maya's hand. No spark this time. "Come on, Maya. It'll be okay."

"I've heard that already today, and it wasn't true."

"Come anyway," Benjamin said. "You have to."

Maya stood and studied Rowan. His hair had fallen over half his face. His mouth was in a straight line.

She glanced past him, toward the outside. She could run, but they knew where she lived. Besides, they knew something about her egg. She didn't know who else to ask.

"My pack," she said. She pointed to her pack, still on Travis's shoulders. Whatever happened, she'd feel better if she could sketch it.

Benjamin eased her pack off Travis's back and slipped the straps over his own shoulders. Travis's gentle snores hitched, then continued.

Gwenda tugged her hand, and Maya followed her and Rowan into the hall.

* TWELVE *

Rowan led them left, away from the front doors, past the wide staircase, and down the corridor toward the center of the building. They passed a pair of glass doors etched with delicate spirals and filigree curlicues. Smoked sunlight shone from the other side, and beyond were dimly visible shapes.

Farther down the hallway, Rowan stopped at a door on the left and knocked.

"Enter," said a voice beyond the door.

Rowan opened the door and stepped through.

The room had a curved, frosted glass ceiling that led to a glass wall at the back. Maya could see blue sky, green lawn, and distant buildings through it, planes of color and shadow, no details discernible.

Maya realized she'd seen the outside of this bubble-like room from her window.

Large, jungly potted plants lined the walls. In the center of the room, three people sat on tufted cushions. The person in the middle was old and tiny, with bushy white hair, black eyebrows, tan skin, and many wrinkles. Maya couldn't tell if it was a man or a woman, only that it liked orange. It was wrapped in a shimmering orange robe.

On either side of Orange Person rested a person in more subdued colors.

"Come in and be seated," Orange Person said. The voice was light as a floating feather.

They entered and thumped down beside each other on the carpet, Benjamin to Maya's left, Gwenda to her right. Rowan closed the door and sat near Gwenda.

"Rowan?" said Orange Person.

Rowan bowed his head. "Great-Uncle Harper."

"Who is your visitor? Why have you called this meeting?"

Maya tugged at her pack. Benjamin eased it off his shoulders and handed it to her.

"This is a neighbor, Maya Andersen, Uncle," Rowan said,

"and something portalwise has happened to her."

Maya slid out her pencil and sketchbook. She flipped to a blank page.

"Please be more specific," Harper said.

Harper had drawn her gaze as soon as she entered the room. When someone or something was so eyecatching she had trouble looking away from it, she always wondered what else was near it that people normally wouldn't notice.

She checked the other people hiding in Harper's light.

On either side of Harper sat a tall, caramel-skinned woman. The two could have been sisters. They wore dark velvet dresses, green melting into brown melting into black. Their gray hair hung in gentle waves around their shoulders. They sat so still birds might land on them, mistaking them for trees.

As she waited for Rowan to answer Harper's question, she quick-sketched the Tree Sisters. Drawing soothed the flutters in her stomach. She didn't know what was going to happen to her, but whatever it was, she could make pictures of it.

"Stranger?" said Harper.

The sisters had widow's peaks. Their light-colored eyes tilted up at the outer edges. Maya drew their faces side by side. One's nose was a little longer. She wore a pendant with a moon that had small, shiny metal triangles dangling from it. The other wore silver star earrings.

Rowan leaned past Gwenda. "What are you doing?" he whispered. Maya glanced at him. He looked even madder than usual.

"What I always do," Maya whispered back.

"Well, stop it! No pictures!"

Maya stilled her pencil and glanced toward him. No pictures? That wasn't going to work—

One of the Tree Sisters leaned closer to Harper and murmured something in his ear. He glanced at her.

Benjamin nudged her. "Maya."

"What?"

"Uncle asked you a question."

"Oh." She bit her lip and looked up. "He was talking to *me*? What'd he say?"

Harper held up a hand. "First, we must attend to something. Rowan, who stands outside the door?"

"What? What else could go wrong?" Rowan scrambled to his feet, then went to the door and opened it.

"What are you doing here?" Rowan asked.

"Following you," said Travis's voice.

"Come in," Rowan said, his voice grouchy. Travis

shambled into the room and Rowan shut the door behind him. "Uncle, this is Travis Finnegan."

"I see. It's a day for visitors. How interesting he found his way here." Harper's voice was dry, maybe sarcastic.

Gwenda jumped to her feet. "How come you're awake?"

Travis smiled and shrugged. "I've been put to sleep by you people before, so I didn't drink very much this time." He flopped to the floor near Maya.

Behind them, Rowan knuckled Gwenda's arm. "Another mistake," he whispered with a frown. "You didn't spell the drink hard enough."

"Stop it," she whispered, pushing his hand away.

"Shh," Benjamin hissed at them both.

"You've been put to sleep by us before, child?" Harper asked.

"Yeah," said Travis. "Oma—my grandmother—is friends with Miss Elia, in apartment 6, and she brought me over here a few times to visit, when she could still get around. Miss Elia was always nice to me. She taught me weird games and gave me ginger cookies. One time I was playing hide-and-seek with the kids in the neighborhood, and I ran inside the building without being invited, and a woman found me and took me into Benjamin's apartment and gave me some chocolate milk. I woke up on the front porch after dark, and I got in lots of trouble for coming home late."

"What is your grandmother's name?" a Tree Sister asked. Her voice was soft and gentle.

"Heidi Orgelbauer."

"I remember her," said the Tree Sister. "She is one of our *giri*."

"What's *giri*?" Maya whispered to Benjamin.

"Humans who help us," he answered almost without moving his lips.

"You have *giri* blood?" Harper said to Travis. "That explains why our wards are weak against you. Where is your grandmother now?"

"At home." Travis's answer was abrupt.

"Hmm," said Harper. "Well, you're on our ground and must abide by our decisions. We'll decide about you later. Now I want to focus on the reason Rowan called this meeting. Girl, what portalwise thing has happened to you?" Harper asked. "Tell me."

Maya didn't want to answer, but she couldn't stop the story flowing out of her as easily as air. "Last night a fairy flew into my room and slept on me," she said. She glanced at Travis, who lifted his eyebrows but didn't say anything.

Maya's mouth kept talking even when she looked away from Harper. She told how the fairy left magic dust on her, how the dust attracted not only Janus House kids but some other boy—she drew a picture and showed it to Harper— and how the boy stuck this egg on her.

"This boy," Harper said. "We already have an alert out on him. We have searchers looking for him now."

"Maya drew us a picture at lunch," Gwenda said. "Twyla brought it home to show to Aunt Columba. That boy said 'chikuvny' to Maya."

"Ah," said Harper. His bushy brows lowered. "Show us the egg, please."

Maya held out her left wrist. The shallow alien dome there glowed with beautiful colors: peacock blue and spring green, scarlet and sulfur yellow. As she stared at it, she thought, *What did Harper just do to me? How could I spill all these details to strangers? I don't like this!*

A red streak flowed across the egg, then a black streak, which spread in swirls to cover the egg; then a flower of red and orange bloomed and faded against the darkness. She felt heat in the egg. Was it hatching?

Travis focused on the egg's changes, too. "Could that thing *be* any weirder?" he muttered.

"Don't ask," Maya whispered.

Gwenda raised her hand. "It's a baby *sissimi*." She held up the book. "There's an entry."

"A *sissimi*!" said a Tree Sister. "The message traffic has been full of news of this! The young *sissimi* are carefully kept, carefully guarded, yet three are missing, and no one knows how. It's a story that took time to get here, Uncle, five portals away. No portal on the *sissimi* world lets unbonded infant *sissimi* through. How could one be here?"

Maya glanced at Gwenda. She hadn't gotten the Janus House kids to define "portal" for her yet, but she knew this: portals were ways to other worlds. Other worlds, Chikuvny Boy, an alien life-form on her arm . . . and people were talking to each other about it. She turned to Travis, wondering how much of their earlier discussion he had overheard. If he had slept through it, this must be even more confusing to him.

He leaned back on his arms, his hands flat on the carpet. He yawned and didn't cover his mouth. How could he be bored?

Harper lifted a steel orb about the size of a tennis ball from the floor. His fingers danced over it, and then he spoke to it. "Who's on communications? Nydia? We need to send out an alert to the general council. More evidence of rogue portals. We have found one of the missing *sissimi*."

"I'll contact them," said a small, clear voice from the orb.

They were broadcasting this to who-knows-where, using a tennis ball–shaped cell phone, talking about Maya's egg as though it were theirs. She hugged the egg to her chest.

Harper set down the steel ball. "Did the boy tell you anything about how he got it, child?"

"He stole her. Some Krithi people told him—"

"Krithi!" cried everybody else in the room in horrified voices.

Ominous silence closed down behind the word.

"Krithi," said Benjamin. He shook her shoulder. "Why didn't you tell us before?" He sounded mad.

"Huh? But I don't know what a Krithi is."

"How could she, *kleek*?" Gwenda knocked Benjamin's hand off Maya's shoulder. "Get some sense."

"Maya," said Harper, "tell us what the boy said."

It happened again. She opened her mouth and words fell out, this time not her own words, but those Chikuvny Boy had said to her. "'I stole her. The Krithi told me how. They said she would be my perfect friend. They told me what *sissimi* grow into. Companions. Collectors. Protectors. The Krithi said I could raise her here, far from her home. Then none of her masters can find me. I didn't know she needs a local host, or she doesn't get the right—'"

Even her voice sounded a little like Chikuvny Boy's, mimicking his slightly odd accent. At first she was surprised that she could remember what he had said word for word. Then she was mad because Harper, tiny Orange Person, was giving her orders, and she didn't have a chance to say no.

Her left wrist burned. She glanced down. The egg was dark, glowing red, with black spots.

She forgot where she was. Worried, she cupped her hand over the egg. Was it dying again?

The egg cooled immediately. When she lifted her hand, the egg was grass green, spotted with yellow colorbursts.

"What are you doing?" she whispered to it. "Are you okay?"

Mad? A tiny voice spoke in her brain.

Astonished, she pressed the egg to her cheek. "Did you say something?" she whispered.

My Other?

"This is much worse than we thought. The Krithi are traveling again," Harper said. He lifted the steel ball and spoke into it.

THIRTEEN

"It will take some time to set up a full council meeting," Harper said when he had finished muttering to the ball. "In the meantime, we should decide what to do about your problem, Maya, and the problem presented by Travis."

"My problem?" She was still struggling with surprise that her egg could talk to her.

"We are sorry that you were drawn into this, through no fault of your own." Harper turned his gaze to Gwenda, who chewed her lip and stared at the floor. "When we make mistakes, we do everything in our power to correct them. There is a chance we can repair the damage and let you get back to your normal life."

"Repair the damage?" Maya said.

"Free you from the *sissimi*, clear the troubling memories from your mind, send you home. Ease you back into the world you know."

"But Uncle—" Gwenda began.

"No. No. No!" Maya jumped up, hugging the egg to her chest. He wanted to take back the magic? He wanted to take away her *egg*? She had lost Stephanie already. She wasn't going to let anyone take this. "You can't have my memories. You can't have my egg. No!"

"The *sissimi* was stolen."

She shook her head. "Not by me. But it's mine now. You can't have it."

"She's right, Uncle," Gwenda said. She held up the big book. "The book says *sissimi* bond for life. The bond is set soon before they hatch. It's Maya's now."

Harper held out a hand, and Gwenda put the book into it. He searched for the entry and read aloud quietly in their foreign language to the Tree Sisters. The only word Maya understood was *sissimi*.

While he read, Maya settled on the carpet and sketched everyone in the room, occasionally pressing the egg against her left cheek for the comfort of its warmth and purr.

Rowan, Benjamin, and Gwenda sat and listened to Harper read, Gwenda fiddling with her charm bracelet. Travis looked asleep sitting up, but he wasn't snoring.

Maya checked her watch. Mom and Peter were likely home already. They might be wondering where she was, although probably not worrying, because there was a five o'clock after-school curfew, and it wasn't five yet.

She got out her cell phone to call and let them know she was visiting the neighbors.

She had no bars.

"That won't work here," Gwenda murmured. "We have a damper against all kinds of electronic signaling, in or out."

Maya looked at the glass ceiling and wall. Was glass enough to interfere with cell transmission? Maybe they had other ways of suppressing things. "What about the steel tennis ball thingy he talked to?"

"Not, strictly speaking, electronic," Benjamin whispered.

"I need to call my family," muttered Maya. "They're expecting me."

"They will have to wait." Harper put down the book and stared at Maya. "This entry does not tell us how to deal with this situation," he said, while Maya thought about her family having to wait. That wasn't fair. They would worry—

"You can't take the *sissimi* away from her," Benjamin said. "That part was clear."

Harper frowned, thumped the book shut. "We need more information. We need to speak with Loostra." He lifted the steel ball again and spoke into it.

"Who's Loostra?" Maya whispered to Gwenda.

"She's a specialist in world-mingling matters."

If there was a specialist in world-mingling matters, it must mean . . .

This happened all the time.

This happened all the time.

Everybody in Gwenda and Benjamin's family knew there were—what? Extraterrestrials? Supernatural creatures?

Travelers.

If only Steph was here! She would have loved this. Maya's spirit soared, then fell. She blinked to clear her eyes, then noticed her left wrist was almost humming. She touched the egg to her ear and heard a soothing buzzing, an egg song of comfort; and she felt suddenly comforted.

Harper stood, and so did the Tree Sisters; Gwenda tugged Maya to her feet, and Benjamin and Rowan rose as well.

Maya was surprised that Harper was only about her height, five feet tall.

Rowan roughly shook Travis's shoulder. Travis snorted and opened his eyes.

"Uncle, does Travis come with us?" Rowan asked.

Harper frowned and stared at Travis, who rolled to his feet. "I'm game," said Travis, "whatever it is."

"You could stay here and take a nap," said Benjamin. "We'll come back for you."

"And miss out on the fun?"

Harper stared at Travis. "That raises a question. Do you consider this fun? We don't usually recruit *giri* so young, but we will make an exception for you. Will you join the *giri*, or should we wash away your memories of this day?"

"Those are my choices? What the heck is a *giri*?"

"*Giri* are our helpers in the outside world. They know and keep our secrets, and they do us necessary services we can't do for ourselves."

Travis's brows drew together. "What the heck could I do that you people can't?"

"Travel outside the range of the portal," Harper said.

"What's the range of the portal?"

Harper exchanged glances with the Tree Sisters. "Perhaps thirty miles," he said. "There is some individual variation. But not much."

"Whoa," said Travis. "Does that mean you guys can't get away from here?"

"Not after we become adult and bond to our specialties," Harper said after a pause. "It is a peculiarity of the Earth portals that they hold us tight. Though I can go through a portal to any place it leads, I cannot go far from it on this side or any other."

Travis frowned. "What kind of special services do you need from—from *giri*?"

"Not as many as we used to, now that we have the Internet," said a Tree Sister, "although we can't use it in the house."

"We could use some help with that," said the other Tree Sister.

"Mostly it involves going somewhere to get us something," Harper said, "or to check out a situation. These tasks will not be yours until you are older. For now, it would mean maintaining secrecy and protecting our affairs."

"Well, good that it doesn't involve more work for me right away. I've already got jobs after school that take up all my time, one of which"—he grabbed Maya's right hand and tilted it so he could look at the face of her watch (no spark; Maya's egg must have recognized Travis as a friend from his first touch)—"I'm totally missing right now, and I'll catch holy hell when I get home. My oma really did stuff like that for you?"

"She did," said the Tree Sister. "She loved to travel. Sometimes she tracked down strays for us, and sometimes she brought us special things we couldn't get for ourselves."

"Oh," Travis said. "Strays? Like that fairy Maya talked about? That explains—the Doowah Box, maybe? Oh. Whoa. And that wand thing? Oma used to point it different directions, and sometimes it would light up. She never let me play with it, though. And she never took it out when Opa was home. Is that—?"

"A seeker," said a Tree Sister. "It can detect *chikuvny*. Very few were made, and we have lost the technology. Does she use it still?"

"She doesn't use much of anything still," Travis said, his voice flat.

"My apologies."

"So I can probably ask if she'll let me return it to you." His voice softened. "We still talk, anyway. About almost everything, except she's never mentioned this secret life she used to lead. Cowabunga. You're offering me a choice between a life where I know what you guys are doing versus a life where

I don't? I'm *so* much more wanting to know. I'll go with the *giri* thing."

"Good," said Harper. "We have not welcomed a new *giri* in a long time. A young one will be good. There are some necessary steps to making you *giri* we will have to take, but right now, we must talk to Loostra about the *sissimi* matter. Come." He strode toward the door. Rowan got there ahead of him and held it open for the Elders.

Maya put away her sketchpad and slipped her pack on. "Where are we going?" Maya whispered to Gwenda.

"To the portal," Gwenda whispered back. "Loostra can't come far from it."

* FOURTEEN *

Rowan led them farther into the building. The corridor turned right, and just past the turn, on the right-hand wall, there was a wide door with no knob. Rowan tapped his fingers against a small square in the center of the door, in a rhythm more complex than an ATM code, and the door opened with a whoosh.

Beyond the door was a landing, and then stairs that led down into a darkness interrupted by halos of multicolored light. Cool, spicy-smelling air rose up the stairwell toward them.

Gwenda took Maya's right hand, and they followed Harper, Rowan, Benjamin, and the Tree Sisters down into darkness, Travis at their heels.

Down the rabbit hole, Maya thought, *where everything works differently and strange is the new normal.* Maya wished Stephanie were here. Steph would have been dancing with excitement. *Why are you so slow, Maya? A new world is waiting!* Maya's throat tightened with missing her.

Sudden anger flashed through her, too. *How could you leave me, Steph? Look at all the stuff you're missing! How can I enjoy it without you?*

The *sissimi* purred against her wrist. *I'm here,* it said.

"You're here," Maya whispered. She pressed the egg against her cheek. Warmth, a shifting movement under her skin, the silent vibration of comfort.

There was a dark maze beneath the Janus House Apartments. Other corridors branched off from the one they were walking. The air changed as they passed by. Sometimes warmer, sometimes colder, it carried scents of cooking, incense, roses, electricity, fire, and many things she'd never smelled before. Everywhere there was the scent of fairy dust. *Chikuvny.*

Rounded doorways opened off the corridor on either side, but most of them were curtained shut. Maya heard strange voices and unknown languages through some of the curtains, and felt heat radiating from others. One curtain was crusted with ice crystals. Another seemed woven of glass strips.

"What *is* all this?" Maya whispered to Gwenda.

"This is where we work. Most of us live upstairs, and the classrooms and kitchen are up there, too. Our real lives mostly happen down here."

"Sunless," Travis muttered from behind them. "Kinda creepy. Like mole rat colonies."

"There's light, but it comes from other places."

Finally they passed a door where a curtain was parted. Maya paused to peek in, and Travis peered past her. Three people sat in darkness, studying windows in the walls. Or were they windows? They were a little like old-fashioned TV screens, or portholes. Maya had a brief shivery thought that they were in a landlocked submarine.

Different moving scenes showed in the portholes: forests of plants Maya had never seen before, spiky cities, mushroomy cities, cities of giant flowers, where people who weren't human flew or crawled or wandered. Skies over the strange landscapes ranged from lilac to lime to lemon, with clouds streaking across them like flotillas of cotton candy, ice crystal scarves, or dark, gritty trails of sand.

"You guys!" Gwenda dragged them away.

They came to another doorway. Harper lifted the curtain and spoke to whoever was on the other side. He said the word "Loostra." Someone said something back. Harper nodded and dropped the curtain before Maya could see past him.

They came to a threshold at the end of the corridor and stopped.

The threshold was about a foot wide, ringed with colored lights. Beyond it was a cavern the size of a basketball court, with other light-ringed entrances around it. The entrances were different sizes. One was so small Maya wasn't sure she could fit through it on her hands and knees. Another stretched up almost to the cavern's ceiling, wide enough for elephants or maybe whales to go through.

"Is that the portal?" Maya whispered to Gwenda, pointing at the circle of lights before them.

Harper turned toward her. "No, child, this is not the portal. Step carefully."

They crossed the threshold one at a time, starting with Harper, followed by the Tree Sisters. Gwenda went before Maya, then turned and looked back. "Be careful," she said.

How could Maya be careful? Try not to trip?

She stepped into the opening. Before she could put her foot down on the other side, something swaddled her in clinging folds of invisible energy and lifted her above the ground, while *zis*sing electric noises snapped in her ears. Her skin fizzed. Suspended midway between the threshold and the top of the doorway, she shivered and shook. She struggled, tried to move her arms and legs, but she was trapped tight, smashed between clear planes, as though she'd been laminated. She tried to scream, but she couldn't even open her mouth.

The egg pulsed against the bones of her wrist, hot, cold, hot, cold, and then scorching.

Something shifted. A streak of heat shot up her arm from the egg, zoomed all through her and out to the tips of her fingers and toes.

The restraints that held her vanished. She fell through into the cavern. Gwenda caught her shoulders before she collapsed, and Travis and Benjamin were there, too, steadying her. "You're all right," Gwenda said gently. "You're all right."

Maya rubbed her eyes, scrubbed her cheeks. The shaking stopped, and she realized she actually felt okay. "What was that?" she said. Her voice came out too high.

Chikuvny smell was very strong here.

"One of our safeguards," said Gwenda.

Benjamin patted her back. "It's kind of like customs, only without the questions. The trap ring activates when contraband comes through."

The others gathered around them.

"So the *sissimi* didn't come through our portal," said the first Tree Sister thoughtfully. "Or it has changed since it arrived."

"What does that mean?" Maya asked. Again, too high.

"Normal humans can walk through the ring without pause," the Tree Sister said and nodded toward Travis. "Your egg snagged you, as it would have snagged anyone carrying it through the other way. Smugglers haven't troubled us in a very long while."

"What shifted?" Harper asked.

"What do you mean, Uncle?" asked the other Tree Sister. "Didn't you shut the trap ring down and release her?"

"No. Something shifted to accommodate the tangle."

They all stared at Maya's wrist. She looked at her egg. It hadn't changed, as far as she could tell. Pink pulsed across it, followed by grass green and Chinese red.

"Hmm. Possibly it did come through our portal." Harper turned to the moon-pendant Tree Sister. "Sarutha, please get me the work logs from the last five days, and ask Nydia to query all other Earth portals for unusual activity in the past—Maya, when did the renegade come here?"

"Renegade?" Maya asked.

"The person who gave you the *sissimi*."

"I don't know," she said. *Little one?* she thought.

Rrr, the egg responded, a growl softening into a purr. How could the egg measure days, when it hadn't even hatched yet? Maya shook her head.

Harper said, "That picture we have of him. You drew it?"

Maya glanced at Benjamin, who nodded.

"I did," she said.

"He looked haggard."

"He was really sick by the time he put the egg on my arm. Much sicker than when I met him in the morning. The sketch is from the morning."

"If local conditions made him sick, five days' backsearch ought to be long enough," Harper said, and he nodded to the Tree Sister, who slipped out through the light-ringed doorway they had just come in.

"Gwenda, call the portal team," Harper said.

"You okay?" Gwenda whispered to Maya.

"I guess." Maya still felt shaky from being trapped by the door. Now Gwenda was leaving. Benjamin stood beside her, though, and he looked reassuring. Travis was a tall presence on her other side, and Rowan stood nearby, though whether that was good or bad, Maya wasn't sure.

"I'll be right back." Gwenda squeezed Maya's shoulder,

then ran through one of the other doorways.

She returned followed by six people, three men and three women, different shapes and sizes and hair colors, dressed in varied clothes. They spread out near the center of the cavern in a ragged circle.

"Is Loostra ready to come through?" Harper asked.

Gwenda nodded, then stood beside Maya. She gripped her own elbows and hunched her shoulders.

The newcomers spread their arms wide. A low hum sounded, making the ground thrum under their feet. The people sang, softly at first, a melody that almost repeated but didn't quite, each time a variation on the time before. They started in unison, and then they split into a multistrand harmony, and the song grew louder. The hum under their feet rose, louder and a little higher, and a streak of fluttering, glowing red appeared in the air in the center of the cavern, within the circle of the portal team. A sheet of green shimmered into sight, followed by a panel of lavender, then orange, blue, yellow-green, scarves and scoops of glowing colored light, weaving around each other, growing denser, curtains and waterfalls and skies of color.

Reflected light danced over the walls. Pale spirals and circles glinted in the smooth, glassy surface of the floor. The air smelled like the scent after a lightning strike, and, inexplicably, like violets, but most strongly of carnation and cinnamon.

Maya slid her pack off and grabbed her notebook and a pencil, then just stood there. This was the most amazing thing she had ever seen, but what could she do about it? *Oh, Steph, if only—*

No way could she capture this without colors. She leaned forward and set her mind on Memorize.

"What is that?" she murmured.

"*This* is the portal," Benjamin whispered.

The hum rose again, the song reached a high chord, all the colored light brightened toward white, and then—

Something long, pale, and jointed scuttled from the center of the ragged rip in the air.

✴ FIFTEEN ✴

One end of it rose up. It had hundreds of small jointed legs fringing its sides. It was flatter than a snake, and it had many body segments. It looked more like a humongous centipede than anything else.

"Wha—wha—wha—" Travis gasped.

Maya clutched Gwenda's arm and tried to drag her toward the door.

Gwenda didn't budge. "Wait," she said.

The top of the thing's body waved in the air. It had six longer limbs at that end, each jointed three times, below a bulging, rounded head. The longer legs curled and unfurled as the portal faded behind it.

A moment later, the cavern was just a cavern again. Plus a giant centipede.

The six people who had conjured up the portal lowered their arms.

Nobody was running away.

The centipede's six long limbs wove gracefully through the air until they all pointed toward Maya. Then they stopped.

"Fetch it," said the centipede. It sounded female.

"Child," said Harper. "Come."

"You're—what? You're—" She didn't even know what to ask. A crazy image of Peter trying to find a jar big enough to hold this creature flashed through her mind.

"Come," Harper said again, in that creepy voice that made her obey, and she walked unwillingly toward the enormous centipede, fear knotting her stomach. Was it going to eat her? Was that how they solved their problems?

"Just a danged minute," said Travis. He came up behind Maya, put his arms around her chest, and lifted her off the ground. Her feet kept walking on air, her heels knocking into his shins. "Somebody tell us this thing is safe!"

"I will not harm you," the centipede said. Its voice sounded warm and comforting, like the best mother in the world. "On the lives of my three hundred children I swear it."

Gwenda said, "It's Loostra," as though that explained everything. "She never hurts people."

"Take the whammy off Maya anyway, and let her get there by herself," said Travis.

There was heat at Maya's left wrist. A shiver ran through her, and her legs stopped kicking. Travis set her down and she stood, uncertain. She twisted toward the door they had come in through, then back toward the center of the cavern, where the giant pale segmented bug from outer space waited, its forelegs curling and uncurling in her direction.

No danger, thought Maya's egg.

"All right," Maya said. She walked toward Loostra, and so did everyone else. Travis stayed even with her, and she glanced up at him and mouthed, *Thanks.*

As they got closer, Maya smelled Loostra: vinegar, damp dirt, a hint of rank, crushed grass.

"This is Loostra," Harper said. "Loostra, this is Maya."

Maya tried to slow her heartbeat; it was shuffling in her ears, and it pulsed through the egg.

Everybody else seemed calm, even Travis, as though he ran into giant talking centipedes every day. She took a deep breath and let it out slowly.

"Maya," said Harper, "and a *sissimi*."

The centipede had a hard round head with six dark velvety spots on it. "Ah," she said, but Maya couldn't tell where she spoke from. "Show me." She sounded like the best mother in the world again, asking to see a scraped knee so she could put a Band-Aid on it.

Maya calmed.

Benjamin nudged her.

"Don't hurt it," Maya said, pressing the egg against her chest and shielding it with her right hand. "Don't take it off."

"What have they told you about me, Maya?" asked the centipede. "Whatever it is, it is wrong. I only ever look at things. I study them. I decide and inform, but I do not *do*."

"You promise?"

"I promise."

Maya edged three steps closer to it. Its vinegar scent was almost overwhelming. She held out her wrist.

It lowered its front end. The six longer limbs reached out and hovered above Maya's egg, then wove through the air around it. "Ahhh," it said. "Beautiful. Ahhh. Rarely have I seen one of these so close." It made soothing, wordless, musical murmurs. "A new variant. Of course. With every new host, a new variant. What an elegant creature it is."

"What do we do with it?" asked Harper.

"Leave it alone." Loostra almost sang her answer.

"But the child is not a traveler," said Harper. "She didn't step into this risk with knowledge. This pairing is wrong."

"Leave it alone," Loostra sang. "There is nothing you can do. They are bonded now, and nothing can change that." Its head turned, aiming its eye spots toward her wrist, one at a time. "Child, may I touch it?"

"You won't hurt it?"

"I won't hurt it."

Maya lifted her wrist higher. One hard-shelled limb drifted down until the very tip touched her so lightly she couldn't feel it. Lemon yellow color formed on the egg and rayed out across all the other colors. Maya felt a weird click under her skin.

Loostra gasped and jerked her leg away.

"Of course it can already defend itself and its host. I should have known," she said. "Thank you, Maya." She turned to Harper. "This answers one part of a complicated question."

Harper nodded. "One *sissimi* we have found. Two more are still lost. And this invasion and theft was orchestrated by the Krithi, or so we believe."

Loostra hissed. "So I had heard—it travels on the info

web—but I had hoped the rumor was wrong."

Harper nodded to Maya. "You heard the boy say 'Krithi'?" he asked.

"You know I did," Maya said. He was the one who had forced her to repeat Chikuvny Boy's words.

"It's the first we've heard of them escaping the interdict," Harper said.

"The monitors are checking the nurseries for evidence, and the Force has been alerted," said Loostra. "You will tell us when you learn more. For now, I am ready to go home."

"How do we handle this situation?" Harper asked, waving toward Maya.

"With reason. With friendship. With family." She dropped her front end and coiled into a spiral. "Thank you for showing me your friend," she said to Maya.

"Have you seen one before?" Maya asked.

"Never in its embryo state."

"What is its other state? What happens when it hatches?" Maya cupped her right hand over the egg.

"It is always different. You will be the first to know."

"Oh," said Maya. "Thanks." *Thanks a lot. Very helpful.*

Loostra uncoiled and clattered back into the center of the circle of six, the portal team. "Farewell."

The team lifted their arms. The hum started again, low and drumming under their feet, and the colors danced in the air. Maya watched, entranced, snapping one mental picture after another.

The colors brightened, then faded, and Loostra was gone.

SIXTEEN

They wound their way back up to the solar room. Harper took the central cushion again, flanked by the Tree Sisters. He gestured to the five young people, who dropped to the carpet in front of him.

Maya unpacked her sketchpad, thinking about Loostra and how to draw her, then checked her watch. Past five o'clock. "Excuse me," she said. "I know things are still messy, but I have to go home now."

"That is not possible," said Harper.

"What?" Maya jumped up, panicked. She grabbed her pack and turned toward the door.

Rowan caught her shoulders. "He doesn't mean you can't *ever* go home," he said.

Heat gathered at Maya's left wrist, arrowed up her arm, cloaked her shoulders. Something crackled. Rowan cried out and released her. His palms were bright red. "Ow! Ow! Ow!"

Maya, ready to run, glanced at her wrist. The egg had gone dark again, with red streaks across it. It was almost growling, an agitation under her skin like water boiling.

"Shh, shh, shh," she whispered, and pressed it against her cheek, her eyes closed. It felt hotter than before, but as she crooned to it, the bubbling against her cheek subsided.

Gwenda had jumped up. She clasped one hand with the other, maybe to stop herself from trying to touch Maya the way Rowan had. "Maya. Tell the *sissimi* we're not threatening you. What the Elder means is we can't let you go until we explain a little more. You'll get home soon. I promise."

Maya lowered her hand and studied her egg bump. The color had softened to a dark, velvety blue, with no red streaks. "We're listening."

Harper sighed, and glanced at the Tree Sisters. They nodded. "Maya," he said quietly, "if we cannot return you to your normal life, we have another way to help. Will you let us make you part of our family?"

"But I have a family already." She thought longingly of

them, remembered how everybody had been at breakfast. Harried, together, irritated, used to each other. It all seemed so far away now, oddly precious.

"You have new problems now, things your other family won't know how to handle."

"I don't even know you. All I know is you keep ordering me around, and I don't like it."

Gwenda touched Maya's sleeve. "Let us make you part of our family. Then we can tell you everything."

"Let us make you part of our family," Benjamin said. "Then you can *travel*." He glanced toward the floor as though he could see all the way down to the portal cavern.

"But I just got here," she said. She had just been uprooted from the place she had spent her entire life and moved to Spores Ferry, which was proving more different from Catspaw, Idaho, than she had ever imagined. She felt totally unready to leave anybody she loved. She just wanted to hold on to her family tighter, stop them from slipping away the way Stephanie had. "I don't *want* to travel."

Although . . . to go through the light—the portal—to other places? Places where skies came in other colors, cities grew spikes, and things that weren't human locomoted over strange streets.

So much to draw.

"You don't have to go anywhere until you're ready," said the moon-pendant Tree Sister. She had a beautiful smile.

Maya stared at her feet, moved them back and forth on the carpet. The shushing noises helped her think. She would have more family, these Janus House people, if they adopted her. She might not make friends with the other kids at school, but she could travel in the JH pack.

She glanced at Rowan, a guy she wasn't sure she'd want for a cousin after seeing the way he treated his family. She didn't think he'd want her for a cousin, either, so she was surprised when he said, "Let us make you part of our family. You're gifted." He nodded toward her sketchpad, which she'd dropped when she jumped to her feet. "We can use that."

Her breath caught in her throat. Rowan sounded grumpy, but he also sounded sincere.

"Though you have to leave those sketches here, the stuff that shows our secret side."

"What?" she said.

"You have to help us keep our secrets. That's what family does."

"If we make you part of our family, it doesn't mean you

lose your own family," said the moon-pendant Tree Sister. "It only means you add ours."

"Does it mean you'll order me around even more than you already have?" she asked Harper.

He smiled. "Probably," he said. "We're the Elders. We have that power. We try to use it only when necessary."

Maya paused, then said, "If people in your family can't travel farther than thirty miles from the portal—I don't—Will I be trapped, too?"

"That won't happen to you, child," said the star-earring Tree Sister. "You are not of our blood. You don't have our restrictions knitted into your bones. You will be our choice child, not our blood child."

"Can't I do the *giri* thing, like Travis? Find out what's going on here and just not talk about it?"

"That's not enough," Harper said. "You have been touched and changed by something that came through a portal, though it wasn't one of ours. Portals are our business. We can't abandon you unhelped. A family tie will give us extra ways to aid you." He sighed and said, "Well, give it some thought. In the meantime, I will take another precaution." He came and knelt in front of her. "Maya, Travis," he said, "stick out your tongues."

They did it. He was being an Elder again: Maya didn't know how *not* to do it. Travis, beside her, opened his mouth, too, and stuck his tongue out, his face a picture of surprise, changing to panic. It was the first time Harper had used command power on Travis, Maya thought. No wonder he was surprised.

Harper tapped each of their tongues with his thumb.

A taste of licorice crossed Maya's tongue, and she felt a prickly shock shoot through her. Harper's hand lifted before the egg could strike back. "There's your silence," he said.

"Huh?"

"Neither of you can speak about what you've seen to outsiders now. Maya, Rowan is right: draw all you like, but leave the pictures here. Travis, we will have a more formal meeting and lay out the articles of *giri* agreement soon. Maya, if you let us make you part of our family, we'll introduce you to all of us and have a welcoming celebration for you . . . after we have a full council meeting about the Krithi, which I will call tonight. We have a lot of work to do."

"What's with these Krithi, anyway?" Maya asked. "Why is everybody so mad at them?"

"Centuries ago, we opened portals to the Krithi home-world. They took over those portals, closed some, and used others to conquer. We didn't have a very organized council then, and we didn't discover what they had done until two generations later, when they had killed or enslaved all the people on their conquest planet. When we found out what they had done, we undid it as best we could, shut their portals, and banned their species from ever traveling portalwise again. It's the worst punishment we know.

"Now it appears they've found a way around our barriers. We need whatever you can tell us about their plans."

SEVENTEEN

"I've told you everything," Maya said.

"You may know more than you know, and your companion might know things as well."

She covered the egg with her hand. How could he question it? He didn't know it could talk. She didn't want him to know. If he knew, maybe he would be able to order the egg around, too.

"We'll worry about that tomorrow. I have another gift I'd like to give you."

Silence was a gift, she supposed, though she still wasn't sure how it was going to work. "Yeah? I don't like your gifts. Can I say no this time?" she asked.

"You may." He reached into the folds of his orange robe,

pulled out something. "It will help if you accept this one, though. Hold out your hand."

"Just show me, okay?" She didn't want him to tap her hand and cast some other kind of spell on her.

He showed her a little ring of braided silver, gold, and copper. "This can connect you to us. Choose a finger for it. You can use it to call us when you need us, and it will tell us where you are."

"A tracker," she said. Like the GPS in her phone, only the Janus House protection stopped the phone's signal from getting out, and nobody could use it to find her while she was inside. If she wore a Janus House tracking device, bossy Elders would know where to find her. Well, if she didn't want them to, she could take it off, same way she could ditch her phone.

He nodded. "A tracker. A key to open doors here." He dropped it into her hand.

It fizzed against her palm, then went quiet. She held it close to her egg. The egg didn't spark or turn dark, so maybe it was okay.

She took a big breath and slid the ring onto the middle finger of her right hand. It fit perfectly.

"Thank you," Harper said. "Travis, we will discuss whether you want one of these when we have our formal meeting." His shoulders relaxed, which made Maya realize he might be as tense about all this as she was. "Maya, this will help until we make you part of our family. After that, we will be connected in other ways. For now, I would like to send Gwenda home with you."

"Why?" Maya wasn't sure how to explain to her parents about bringing a guest home on her first day of school. Nobody in her family did that, although they were a guest-friendly household. Everybody needed time to settle into their new routine.

Plus, it felt more like Harper was sending a spy, rather than a friend.

"We don't know much about *sissimi*, but we have learned this much: The *sissimi* has bonded to you. It bonds close to its hatching time. We have no clear information on what the hatching entails, but the event is imminent," Harper said. "Wouldn't you like some help when that happens?"

"Yes," said Maya. "Oh, yes." Her right hand covered her egg, a gesture that was becoming a habit. She had forgotten that she wasn't going to have the egg on her arm forever.

The egg gave a sleepy purr. She peeked under her hand and saw that it had turned rose red, with small yellow flowers.

"Gwenda?" Harper said. "Are you ready for this task?"

"Yes, Uncle. Well, I need my bag."

He smiled and stood. He waved a hand. "You may go."

At least it wasn't an order, Maya thought, repacking her sketchpad.

Rowan stopped her and held out his hand.

She glared at him.

"I'll keep it safe for you. You can have it back as soon as you get here," he said, and for once he didn't look mean or angry, just serious.

She sighed and handed him the sketchpad.

Gwenda and Benjamin led Travis and Maya back to Benjamin's apartment.

Maya was tired and hungry again. It was almost six P.M., way past curfew.

"I know it's late. I'll be right back." Gwenda left.

Benjamin, Travis, and Maya stood in Benjamin's living room.

"Um," said Maya.

"First day of school. Epic," said Travis. "This year is *so* going to be different."

"I'm sorry you got such a rough start," Benjamin said to Maya. "It's probably not what you want to hear, but I'm glad you sat with us, Maya."

She tried out a smile. It felt almost natural.

"Gotta go," said Travis. "I'm way beyond late, and now I have a *ton* of things to talk over with Oma. I wonder if that tongue thing the old dude did to us will mess that up. See you tomorrow." He waved and strode out just as Gwenda returned. She had a bulging tapestry bag over her shoulder.

"Wait, Travis!" Benjamin called. Travis paused with his hand on the knob of the entrance door. "You have to clean up before you leave. Jump up and down on this." He pointed to a thick, woven, bristly mat to the left of the double doorway. "You have to do this every time you leave the building, if you've been below."

"I'll show you." Gwenda stepped onto the mat, shuffled her feet, shook out her skirts, shirt, and shawl, then combed her fingers through her hair. Particles of gleaming, fragrant dust dropped to the carpet and vanished. A very localized breeze swept around her, drawing even more gilt dust from her clothing. "Do the stop, stomp, and shake. It's how we leave the *chikuvny* at home."

Travis looked down at his jeans and T-shirt, shrugged, then stepped onto the mat. The wind lifted his hair. "Stellar," he said, trying out dance moves or maybe martial arts stances before brushing his hands over his shoulders, chest, and legs.

Maya looked at the sleeves of her hoodie. Not much

fairy dust. She stepped onto the mat when Travis stepped off, and slapped her jeans, shook her backpack. The mat sucked air and gold dust down into itself. "Whoa!" Maya said, dancing.

"Maya!" cried Mom as Maya and Gwenda came in through the kitchen door, which was unlocked, to Maya's relief.

Maya shoved her left hand into her pocket and cradled her egg against her side.

"Where have you been?" Dad demanded. "We were about to call the police!"

"Candra's out looking for you right now," Mom said.

"I'm sorry. I'm sorry," Maya said.

"Maya got sick on the way home from school and stopped at my house," said Gwenda. "I'm Gwenda, and I live next door." She waved toward Janus House. "We were closer, and my aunt's a doctor."

"You're sick?" Mom came and felt Maya's forehead. "You don't have a fever. Are you all right now?"

"I think—"

"What happened?"

"I—" Her eyes heated. Tears spilled.

"Did someone hurt you? What happened?" Mom hugged her. Dad came and put his arms around her, too.

"I think I'm okay now. I'm so sorry I'm late."

"But you're okay?" Dad asked.

Maya rubbed her eye with her right fist and nodded. "I'm better now."

"When you didn't call—" Dad said.

"I know. I'm sorry. I'm sorry."

"She did try to call. Our house has a tin roof. No cell service, and most of us don't have phones," said Gwenda. "If it happens again, I'll send one of my cousins over to let you know where she is."

"Did your aunt say what was wrong with her?" Mom asked.

"A blood sugar and stress thing, nothing serious or permanent."

"Stress? Oh, honey, I thought you were finished with—"

Maya was stunned by how good a liar Gwenda was. She realized Mom must be thinking about how sad, angry, and distracted Maya had been last spring and summer. Sometimes she slept for twelve or thirteen hours. Other times she would be going along fine, and suddenly she would stagger, remembering that Stephanie was gone. Tears had come when she was in the middle of singing some song Stephanie had loved and used to harmonize with, or in response to a stupid ad on TV. How strange grief had been, ambushing her at random moments.

The egg purred. She wondered what color it was now, but she couldn't look. She felt reassured and calmed by the gentle vibration.

"Guess not," Maya said to her mother.

Peter rushed in from the dining room. "You're here!" he said.

"Yep. Sorry I'm late."

"I set the table. It's your turn! You get to do it tomorrow instead of me!"

"Will do," said Maya. "Thanks, Peter."

Dad called Candra's cell phone to let her know Maya was home.

Mom finally released Maya.

"Mom, this is Gwenda Janus," Maya said. "She's in some of my classes. Gwenda, my mom, Liz, and my dad, Drew. My little brother Peter, the one who likes animals."

"I remember. Nice to meet you, Peter, Mrs. Andersen, Mr. Andersen," Gwenda said. She shook hands with Maya's parents.

"Can Gwenda stay for supper?" Maya asked.

Mom turned to Dad, and one of those looks passed between them where Maya knew they were talking without words. They smiled at each other and nodded. "All right," said Mom. "Hurry and wash up. Supper's ready. We'll eat as soon as Candra gets back. I'll go set another place."

Maya led Gwenda toward the downstairs bathroom, but Gwenda said, "Can I see your room?"

"Huh? Okay." Maya headed up the staircase, and Gwenda followed. "Hey, can you eat our food? I didn't have a chance to ask."

Gwenda nodded. "Sure. We just have to eat some food spiced with *palta* every day—travelers' spice—to keep us healthy as things come through the portal, and I had some *palta* at lunch. Now you've had some, too."

Maya pressed her hand to her belly, thinking of vinegar soup and pound cake.

"And a good thing, too," Gwenda murmured, glancing along the upstairs hallway. They were alone. "Great-Uncle Harper didn't even ask. He took you and Travis down to the portal without knowing whether you'd been immunized."

"Immunized?"

"Sure. More things come through the portals than the people we're transporting. Air. Insects. Microscopic creatures.

Energies. Other stuff. The trap rings catch most of it, but we have to be careful."

"Did Travis get any, uh, *palta*? He didn't eat."

"It was in the root beer, too." Gwenda smiled. "There's a little in everything we make. He didn't drink much root beer, but he got some. Enough."

Maya opened the door to her bedroom. She wished she'd picked up the room this morning, but who knew visitors were coming? Yesterday's clothes lay on the floor by the closet, along with a couple of shirts she'd tried on last night before settling on the one she was wearing. The desk was a mess, art stuff scattered all over it. She hadn't made her bed.

Gwenda didn't look at any of that. She studied the floor. There was a throw rug by Maya's bed and another next to the bookcase, but most of the floor was varnished wood.

Gwenda went to the bookcase and turned back the rug. "May I make a portal here?"

"What?"

"This is what I'm good at." Gwenda straightened, stared into Maya's eyes, then looked toward the window, her head tilted. "My best skill so far." She spoke without looking at Maya, and her voice sounded toneless. "I can make little local portals."

"Really? How does that—I mean, how?"

Gwenda shrugged, still facing away. "It's the family business. It's been bred in our blood since ancient times to have some kind of skill that applies to portalkeeping. It's in the air we breathe at home—*chikuvny*—and it's in the *palta* that spices our food, the dust of other worlds with a touch of the in-between. We study every skill until a particular aptitude shows up. Mine came early. It's not the skill I would have chosen."

Maya wondered why Gwenda sounded sad. "You can . . . can you open a portal to anywhere you like?"

"No. Not yet. Maybe not ever. It depends on how strong my skill gets. Right now, the shorter the distance, the easier I can do it, and it helps if the other end leads home. There's all kinds of energy to draw on there."

Maya went to the dresser and picked up a picture of her and Stephanie when they were six, grinning and showing off their missing teeth. "You can do magic. You know how much my friend Stephanie wanted to be able to do magic? How can you be sad about something so amazing?"

Gwenda joined Maya by the dresser. She looked at the picture of Maya and Stephanie and smiled. You couldn't help it, Maya thought. Steph's grin was so wide. Gwenda peered at the other pictures. "Wow. You guys are always together," she said. "Where is she?"

Maya set the picture back on the dresser. "She died last spring. Cancer." The hollow place opened up in her chest again, grief lying in ambush. She hugged herself and bent her head, falling inward where loneliness waited.

Golden threads wove through the darkness, spinning a face against the absence of light. It was not Stephanie's face. Maya closed her eyes and tried to bring it into focus, but it remained blurred. Something clicked—the egg was humming at her wrist—and she saw, suddenly, that the face belonged to Chikuvny Boy, not the way she had seen him, but some way that represented who he was. A face more felt than seen, something a blind person might create to stand for a treasured person. A flurry of unknown but almost familiar feelings feathered through her.

"Oh, little one," she said, cradling the egg against her chest. It felt cold, and its quiet song was full of loss. Egg had loved Chikuvny Boy, its almost-twin, and lost him.

They mourned together.

Maya remembered the breathing exercises the counselor had taught her, deep, slow, banishing breaths to lift her out of the pit. *Come*, she thought to the egg. *We can't stay down here.*

Don't want to stay. It comes with me when I leave.

I know.

Not alone. Have you.

Have you, Maya echoed. She rubbed her eyes and turned to Gwenda.

"I'm so sorry, Maya," Gwenda said.

"Me, too." Maya stroked the egg, which had turned dark. Gradually it warmed under her fingertips, and green streaks patterned it. "Well, anyway."

"Yes," said Gwenda. "Anyway, I want to open a portal for you here so when the egg hatches, you can come home, and we can take care of you."

"That would be good, I guess," Maya said.

Gwenda rose and went to the door, frowned at the keyhole. "Can you lock it?" she asked.

Maya shook her head. "No, and I sure want to! Peter keeps coming in without asking."

"I can manage it." Gwenda tapped her fingertips against the metal plate with the keyhole in it and sang a soft musical phrase. The lock thudded home.

"What?" said Maya. She came closer. "How did you— can you teach me that?"

"I don't know. It's one of my portalkeeping talents, so probably it's not something everybody can do." She headed back to the rug by the bookcase, where she took off her bracelet and considered it. The charms were round, flat stones about the size of dimes, tan and beige and charcoal, ocher and brick red, with strange, filigreed writing on them. Gwenda selected a rose-gray stone and detached it from the ring. She used it to trace a three-foot-wide circle on the floor, then pressed it into the center of the circle, where it sank into the wood like an embedded jewel.

Gwenda placed one hand over the stone and put the other on top of the first. She sang a short song in the language of Janus House. Her singing voice was low, rich, and melodic. The tune asked a question that made Maya want to answer, though she didn't know what it meant.

Gwenda lifted her hands. The stone and the circle around it glowed foxfire green, then faded.

"Maya," she said and patted the floor beside her. Maya knelt. Gwenda pressed Maya's palm to the stone. Gwenda sang again, the same phrase repeated, then reversed. Maya hummed along, and Gwenda nodded encouragement. The stone heated under Maya's hand. She felt drifty, as though gravity had lost its grip on her.

Heat pulsed at her left wrist, shot up her left arm and down her right arm. Something shoved her hand up, away from the stone.

"What?" said Gwenda.

Maya looked at her right hand. A spiky-rayed star was printed in pink against her palm. "I don't know. It came from the egg."

"The *sissimi* is a protector," Gwenda muttered. "Why would it protect you against being tuned to a local portal?"

Little one?

It wants to take you elsewhere.

That's the point.

Can't be sure it's safe. A storm of sensations washed over Maya—terror, pain, hunger, a wrenching at the core. The fragmenting of a bond—

Maya sat back, stroking the egg. The egg had been through some kind of portal with Chikuvny Boy. Or maybe this was just another way it felt about having lost him. She knew the feeling. She shook her head at Gwenda.

"Well, if I can't tune you to come to me, I'll come to you, or someone else will," Gwenda said.

She dropped the throw rug over the circle and the stone and stood up.

"That's it?"

"That's all I need for now. Except a way for you to summon us." Gwenda took Maya's right hand, and frowned down at the ring Harper had given her. She stroked it with her fingertip. It tingled. "If you need one of us, turn your ring around three times. Someone will come."

"Thanks," said Maya.

Gwenda went to the door and tapped the lock open.

Maya rummaged in her closet and found one of her father's old extra-large NORTH IDAHO—NO SMALL POTATOES sweatshirts. The sleeves were nice and long. She tugged the cuff down over the egg and half over her hand, then checked her appearance in the mirror. The sleeves were baggy enough to hide everything.

Knocks sounded on the door, and then Peter barged in. "Hey, Maya!" he yelled. "When the heck are you coming down? Everybody's home and hungry now, and supper's past ready!"

"How many times do I have to tell you not to come in before I say 'Come in'?" Maya cried. A second earlier and the door would have been locked, and how could she have explained that? What if Gwenda hadn't locked the door, and Peter had come in and seen Gwenda making magic, or seen the egg? "Hey, Dad, can I get a lock for my door?" she yelled as she and Gwenda clattered down the stairs in Peter's wake.

During supper, Maya's family talked about their day.

Candra's journalism teacher was great and had written articles for national magazines, but the school newspaper's editor was an idiot. "I went to the library during lunch and read some back issues. She was editing it last year, too. Talk about boring."

"You going to turn that around?" Dad asked.

Candra grinned. Then she frowned. "Is it just me, or is Jefferson High School really cliquey? It wasn't like that back home."

"Because you were always in the best cliques already," Maya said. She wolfed a piece of chicken, still hungry, even after stuffing herself at Janus House. She dug into her mashed potatoes and gravy. Every bite tasted great. Under the table, she cupped her hand over the egg. It was purring.

Candra glared at her.

Dad smiled. "Maya's right, Candra. You've always been a member of a strong group. You'll find your way here; it's not much different from our old school. I have my work cut out for me, getting those kids interested in history, but I like my classroom."

"I wish Adele were here," Candra said. She had left her best friend behind. She hadn't wanted to move.

"You can still e-mail her," Maya said.

Candra narrowed her eyes at Maya, then looked at her plate. "Yeah, yeah," she muttered.

"Well, the kids in my class are great," said Mom.

"You always say that," Candra said.

"And it's always true. One of the boys—you'd like him, Peter—" She told a story about a boy who brought his pet snake to school wrapped around his neck. Chaos ensued when one of the girls spotted it, and then the boy taught everyone snakes weren't slimy or scary.

Maya glanced around the table at the platter of fried chicken, bowls of salad and mashed potatoes, pitcher of milk, butter dish, and brightly colored plates full of food. Her sister, her brother, her mom, her dad, talking, eating, waving their hands, smiling like this was the best part of their day. It was all so . . . normal. So nice.

Gwenda, silent and smiling, looked different from the rest of them. Her friend. Not yet part of the new normal.

"My classroom has hamsters," Peter said. "Mr. Garcia says I can help him take care of them."

Everybody looked at Maya.

Her big news of the day? She met a boy from another planet. He stuck an alien vampire egg on her. She got so sick she thought she'd die, and a boy she hardly knew rescued her. She met new neighbors who had a portal under their house that opened into fairyland and other planets and who knew where else. They wanted to adopt her.

She swallowed and said, "I spent the day without a map. It was really confusing, but I made new friends."

Mom and Dad exchanged a look and a smile again.

"We have lots of classes together," Gwenda said. "I hope Maya's a better student than I am. I could use some help with math."

"Maya's no good at math," Peter said.

"Oh, okay. Maybe we can confuse each other," Gwenda said, and smiled at Maya.

After supper, Maya walked Gwenda home, with Dad watching from the Andersens' front porch. "Thanks for rescuing me," Maya said as Gwenda stepped onto the porch stairs at Janus House. The night was soft and cool around them.

Gwenda smiled, with an edge of sadness. "It's nice to know someone new. I hope we'll be good friends." She held out her right hand, palm up, too high for a handshake.

"I don't—" Maya said.

"Put your hand out like this," said Gwenda. Maya held out her open hand, palm up, and Gwenda slid her fingers across Maya's fingers as though they were pulling away from a handclasp. "This is one of the greetings we do," Gwenda said, "for hello and good-bye." She sighed. "So much happened today."

"Yeah."

"See you tomorrow."

Maya held out her hand again, and Gwenda brushed fingers with her.

Maya's family worked on homework together in the living room after supper—the kids doing it, the parents devising it or correcting it. When they finished, Dad and Peter turned on the TV to watch sports.

Maya went upstairs and changed into her sleepshirt. She wanted to think through the whole day the way she worked best—on paper. She cleared off her desk and set up the colored pencils and watercolors, got a jar of water for her brushes, opened a different sketchbook with heavyweight paper, and started work.

First she made her family at supper. She put golden color

across the page, then drew faces and food on top of the gold so it almost looked like a picture by firelight. She drew everybody laughing.

Then she did three pictures of the portal. She swept washes of color across the page, then penciled in dark silhouettes of the portalkeepers with their arms stretched against the storm of colors. She couldn't get it to look exactly right, but she got some pictures she liked.

She added some quick sketches: Gwenda's profile as she turned away from Maya to look out the window; Rowan's half-face, frowning; and Benjamin's crooked grin. She drew a serious Travis, one she hadn't seen at school.

Then she focused her bendy-neck light on her egg.

The egg changed all the time. Every different thing it did enchanted her. She touched it, and colors flowed around her fingertip. She felt something warm and damp brush against the inside of her skin.

Her egg. Nothing she had planned to get, hers by pure luck, hers in some way she couldn't understand. She made another picture. She couldn't catch the colors; they moved too fast; but she got some pictures that gave a feeling of what her egg looked like between one change and the next.

She called up from memory the drawings she'd made in

her carry-along sketchpad of the Janus House people. Moon and Star Tree Sisters—did she want them for aunts? She liked them, especially Moon, much better than she liked Great-Uncle Harper. Cousin Benjamin. Cousin Gwenda. Cousin Rowan. All the others she'd seen, off and on, going in and out of Janus House and working in the tunnels below. She dug out an earlier sketchpad and studied the pictures she'd drawn the week before of them playing music, playing games on the lawn, sitting on their porches reading or knitting or swinging. Dark faces, light faces, something similar in the bone structure of most of their faces.

Her new family?

All those times she went to Stephanie's house, or Stephanie came to hers, as though they had two homes and were comfortable in either. She could imagine running up the steps and barging into Janus House as though she belonged there. All those other rooms and apartments. Would she be welcome in them? What else was underground? Maybe she'd be able to look behind all the curtains.

That was, if she consented to become part of the family.

Great-Uncle Harper talked as though there were no other option.

What if she said no?

They would help her with the egg anyway, she was sure. It was portalwise. Once that problem was solved, if there was any way to solve it, would they bar her from ever coming back to Janus House? What if there was some way to take away her memories? From what they'd said, they could do that.

She thought about her mother and father smiling at each other because they thought Maya had made new friends and come up out of the pit she'd lived in since Stephanie died. It was great to see them so happy.

Joining the Janus House family would make everybody over there at least acknowledge her, right? Even if she wasn't their favorite relative. She'd have a whole passel of new friends, sort of, which might build a lot of parental smiles.

She imagined the Andersens and the Janus House clan having a barbecue on the lawn between their houses. It made her laugh.

She felt ready to say yes to Harper when he asked her again.

Before she went to bed, she brought two small sofa pillows to her room. She lay on her back and put one pillow outside her left arm and the other between her arm and her body. If she started to roll over in her sleep, the pillows would wake her up before she squashed the egg.

She turned out the light, closed her eyes, and concentrated on the way the egg felt on her wrist. Warm, vibrating in a silent purr.

She moved each finger of her left hand, felt them respond. The egg had scared her, but it hadn't crippled her.

There was a little live thing inside her egg, a being struggling to be born. A little live thing that had gone through hard times, almost dying. Maybe it had been in pain when the boy gave it to her; maybe it had been hurt as much as she had when it sucked under her skin. She knew it missed Chikuvny Boy. Maya wasn't its first friend.

"You aren't my first friend, either," Maya whispered, stroking her fingers over the egg. "I hope we'll be best friends, though."

She woke when she tried to roll over one of the pillows she had used to brace her left arm. She checked the egg. It was safe.

The orange streetlight on her ceiling was gone; sun shone there instead. She glanced at her alarm clock and saw it was almost six A.M. Her stomach growled with hunger, and her mouth was dry.

She struggled to her feet and went down to the kitchen. The only sound was the refrigerator's hum. After gulping down a couple of glasses of water, she microwaved leftover potatoes and chicken. "Boy, if I'm this hungry now, I better pack a big lunch," she muttered. She made three peanut-butter-and-jelly sandwiches and added three apples, a big bag of carrots, and two Twinkies twin packs.

The stretched skin over the egg was no longer velvety soft, more dry and hard.

Little one?

Still hungry, it thought.

She ate two rolls with butter. Her stomach stopped complaining.

She was supposed to have P.E. today. She wasn't sure what sport, but she had her P.E. uniform, and it wasn't going to cover the egg. What did she have that would? There was that green blouse with the full pirate sleeves, the one that would make her look like the ultimate dork.

Better a dork than a hospital patient.

Probably.

She couldn't possibly go to P.E. with the egg on her arm. Maya wondered if Gwenda's aunt actually *was* a doctor and could write her a medical excuse. Worth a try. First she had better get dressed and ready for school, though, before everybody else was up and could ask her awkward questions.

Fifteen minutes later she was dressed, the pirate sleeves plenty roomy enough to cover anything that might have attached itself to her arms, and she had a fresh sketchbook in her backpack, along with the books and homework she thought she'd need for today. Keys, she thought, and went back for them. Then she went back to get her cell phone from the charger. She raced down the stairs and bumped into her father in the kitchen.

"Whoa! Up early! Nice change from yesterday. What do you want for breakfast?" he asked.

Maya grabbed the big bag lunch she had left on the counter. "I already ate."

"I noticed somebody did, but I assumed it was Peter." He pointed to the pile of chicken bones on the plate by the sink.

"Oh! Sorry!" She threw out the bones, rinsed off the plate, and stuck it in the dishwasher.

"Are you all right?" her father asked.

"Yes. Feeling much better. I have to go next door and ask Gwenda's aunt something, though." She stood on tiptoe to kiss him, then headed for the door.

"What was that streak that went by?" her mother asked her father as Maya closed the front door behind her.

* EIGHTEEN *

Sully was out in the backyard. He usually slept with Peter, who let him out very early and went back to sleep. "Hey, boy," Maya said, going to the fence.

Sully growled at her.

"What?" she said.

The egg vibrated against her wrist. *Something wants to hurt you?*

"No!" Not Sully. She'd known him since he was a pale golden puppy.

Sully growled some more, his tail between his legs, and backed away, his gaze on her left wrist.

"He knows you're there," Maya whispered, shaken.

I won't let him hurt you.

"He doesn't want to hurt me. He wants to hurt you." Maya pressed the egg against her chest, cupping her other hand over her left wrist to protect it. "Spooky."

A minute later, Maya was knocking on the big front door of Janus House. No one answered. She looked around for doorbells or mailboxes or any way of getting someone's attention. Nothing. She could go along the porch and knock on some of the apartment doors, she guessed, but what if she ran into people who didn't know her? Maybe they'd give her drugged root beer first and ask questions second.

She tried the knob. The door opened. The corridor was empty. She walked to Benjamin's apartment door and knocked.

A surprised woman opened the door. She was short and solid, with light brown skin and masses of wavy black hair. Her eyes were black and bright. She wore a yellow terry cloth bathrobe. "*Kiri kara!* Who are you, and how did you get inside?"

"I'm Maya from next door. Is Benjamin here?"

"Oh. Maya!" said the woman. "We've been hearing about you. But how did you get through the wards?"

Benjamin, fully dressed, appeared behind the woman. "Maya. Is everything all right?"

Twyla, buttoning her shirt, peered past her mother's shoulder. "Maya! Hi!" she said, and then vanished.

"Is one of your relatives really a doctor?" Maya asked Benjamin. "I need an excuse to get out of P.E."

"That would be me," said the woman, straightening. "Sapphira Porta, M.D. What's the problem?"

"Ma," Benjamin said in an exasperated tone.

She turned to him, eyebrows up. He tapped his left wrist and nodded toward Maya.

"Oh," she said. "May I see?"

Maya unbuttoned the cuff of her sleeve and turned it back. The egg was flashing many different colors this morning: buttercup yellow, orange, red, sky blue. *You're happy*, Maya said.

We ate. I'm not hungry. I feel good!

"Oh," said Dr. Porta in a different tone of voice. "I always wondered what those looked like before they hatched. Nice. Let me get my prescription pad." She went back into the apartment.

"How'd it go last night?" Benjamin asked.

"Almost normal," Maya said. A shiver ran through her as she stared down and buttoned her cuff, concealing the egg. She wasn't sure why she felt sad. She glanced up at him through her lashes, and then she knew. "Everything's different, and no one noticed."

He sighed, gave her a rueful smile. "Come on in. I'll make you some cocoa." He headed for the kitchen, and she followed. "Have a seat."

She slid out of her backpack and lowered it to the floor, then sat at the table. "The cocoa won't do anything weird to me, will it?"

"Nope." He poured some milk in a pan and put it on the stove, then turned on the gas burner.

Someone knocked. Benjamin lifted his head, turning toward the sound. His eyebrows drew together above his nose. "Now, how—" He went to answer the door and came back with Travis following him.

"No root beer this time," Travis said, "okay?"

"Yeah, yeah." Benjamin spooned chocolate powder into three mugs, then poured a little warm milk in them, stirred, and poured more. He set the mugs on the table with spoons still in them. "Drink up. We have to head out in a couple minutes." He gave his own mug a brisk stir, then drank.

"How's the bump?" Travis asked Maya.

"Happy. It's weird. It's not like it's huge or anything, but I'm still eating for two." Maya stirred and sipped. Rich, dark, warm chocolate. She felt better. The egg purred. She wondered if it could taste what she tasted.

Dr. Porta entered the kitchen from a door on the far side and stopped on the threshold to stare at Travis, who, having watched Benjamin and Maya drink their cocoa without ill effect, was finally tasting his own.

"Another one? Somebody's not doing their job," she said.

"Ma," Benjamin said, exasperated. "And anyway, this is Travis, who's going to be our new *giri*."

"Oh." She blinked, then came to the table and lowered herself into a chair. She had a pad of paper in one hand and a pen in the other. "Maya, tell me your whole name so I can make it official."

"Maya Andersen." Maya spelled her last name, and Dr. Porta wrote her a note, then handed it to her with a flourish.

"Thanks so much," said Maya. She tucked the note in her pocket, took her empty mug to the sink and rinsed it, then put on her backpack. Benjamin and Travis rinsed out their mugs, and they all left.

"Do we have to stomp?" Maya asked Benjamin in the front hall.

He glanced at the mat. "Not if you haven't been underground."

The whole lunchtime crowd of Janus House middle schoolers was waiting on the front porch when Travis, Maya, and Benjamin left the building. They fell into step, the Janus House kids talking to each other, half of the chatter in the other language, half in English.

"Nice shirt," Gwenda told Maya.

"Arrr, swabby," Maya said, roughening her voice. "Scupper the bilgewater and skunnel the skinks."

"What?" asked Gwenda.

"Avast," said Travis. "Stap me for a scurvy dog, ye poltroon!"

"What? What?" Gwenda looked back and forth between them. Maya found herself laughing; she couldn't stop. She loved that she and Travis shared a fake language the Janus House kids didn't know. She laughed all the way to homeroom, and then she settled into her seat between Benjamin and Travis, breathless, and school happened, and only occasionally did she remember her otherworld passenger.

Like at lunch, when she ate everything she had packed and then stared pitifully at the Janus House kids' lunches until Benjamin and Twyla gave her some of their soup and half of their softbread. After that feast, her egg was so happy it purred like a silent powerboat and almost put her to sleep.

Travis spent lunch with his eighth-grade buddies again, but he fell into step with Maya as they headed for social studies.

"Hey, did you talk to your grandmother?" Maya asked him as they dodged down the hall between other students.

"Couldn't. Tongue wouldn't work. I hate that. Did you try to tell anybody?"

"No," she said.

"It's really strange. You open your mouth and your throat closes up. It kinda hurts."

"Yuck."

"I hope I can get the old dude to change it."

"Yeah," Maya said. "Yuck!"

Ms. Rupert, the P.E. coach, accepted her note with raised eyebrows and a glance toward Benjamin and Gwenda. Maya spent gym period sketching on the bleachers.

Benjamin, Gwenda, and Rowan waited for her when she left school, and Travis fell into step with them a little way down the street.

"I'm not sure you're supposed to come today," Rowan told Travis.

Travis shrugged. "My first job starts at four every afternoon, which means I've got a little time to kill. Might as well stop by and see if Uncle Dude wants to mess me up some more."

"He will for sure if you call him that," said Rowan.

"Oh, yeah?" said Travis.

"He doesn't tolerate disrespect."

"We should have an interesting future together, then," Travis said.

Maya leaned closer to Rowan, studying the half of his face she could see. Was Rowan . . . smiling?

"Enter at your own risk," he said, and held open the front door.

Instead of taking a left and entering Benjamin's apartment, Rowan led them on the route they had taken the day before, past other doors and the staircase to the etched glass double doors facing the Y where the corridor forked. Again smoked sunlight came through the frosted glass, and again Maya saw blurred blotches that might be trees or bushes, but today there were things moving beyond the glass, and faint cacophony.

"*Kesa navi*," Rowan said as he turned the doorknob of the right-hand glass door, and the others repeated it. He opened the door and a wall of stench rolled toward them, an acrid beetle-crunch smell combined with burned gunpowder, jasmine, window-washing fluid, and roasted meat. This combined with a discordant assault of piercing sound: human conversation, song—bird, human, insect—the screech of metal on metal, high-pitched peeping, and lower froggy *grunk*s.

"Council's still in session," said Benjamin.

Maya looked past him at a mosaic of strangeness. She couldn't sort it out, not with all the sounds and smells.

"Whoa," Travis said, holding his nose. "Don't know if I can face that without puking." He blinked, his eyes tearing up. "Oh, my God, what is that smell? Is that person glowing? My eyes hurt. I can't—" He turned and backed away.

Rowan closed the glass door, silencing most of the noise and odors, and followed Travis. "We're bred for dealing with this, and we eat food that helps us, too," he said. "We should start you on some softbread and see if it helps."

"I want to see what's in there," Travis said, and coughed, then sneezed, then coughed again. "*Boy*, do I want to see it!

And hear it, and everything else, but I so hit overload. Guess I'll have to wait."

"Do you need to leave right away?" Rowan asked. "Let us get Maya introduced to the council, and then we'll get back to you. There are things we need to talk over today if we can."

Travis checked his watch. "I've got maybe forty minutes before I need to leave."

Rowan opened a door halfway down the hall. "This is my family's place. Hey, Kallie. Could you get Travis a snack? Something with *palta* in it?"

"Uh—" said a voice from within. "Okay."

"That's the food additive that helps us deal with portal-wise stuff. We give it to all our *giri*. Wait for us as long as you can," Rowan said to Travis. "Please."

"Sure," said Travis. He sneezed again and went into the apartment.

"Maya, are you all right?" Benjamin asked as Rowan went back to the door.

Maya coughed. The smells still scraped against her nose and throat. "I don't know."

"She had *palta* yesterday," Gwenda said. "It takes a while to build up in the body, though."

"Let's try," said Rowan. "Great-Uncle Harper specifically

asked us to bring you." He opened the door again and stood to the side, letting her see into the room.

Before her was a courtyard ringed by the walls of the apartment house, roofed by gold-tinted glass that turned the blue sky slightly green and gilded the clouds. In the courtyard, plants and trees grew, some familiar, some so strange she knew they came from Somewhere Else.

In the center of the courtyard was a ring of tables, and at the tables sat many kinds of creatures. There were several that looked like basketball player–sized dinosaurs, and one that was a white lump of something jiggly with deep dents that moved around. Bubbles of golden gas encased some of the others, who were indistinct through the haze but appeared to have many slender limbs and no obvious heads. There were two giant centipedes; Maya knew somehow they were not Loostra. On one of the tables sat something that looked like a small planet with its own atmosphere, continents, and oceans. Benjamin's mother was talking to it.

Spaced around the many creatures were plates and trays and cups and bowls and other strange dishes of what was probably food and drink. Some of the contents steamed, some sizzled, some moved.

The smells and sounds attacked her nose and ears.

The egg, so quiet most of the day, woke and quivered on her wrist. She felt several little jabs in her arm, bright darts of pain. A flush of heat and cold ran through her, and then she could breathe easier and things didn't smell so bad. The sounds smoothed out, too; she didn't think she'd lose her hearing immediately anymore.

Maya opened her pack and rummaged for her sketchpad and pencil.

Rowan gripped her arm. "Not now," he said, and then snatched his hand back. "Ouch!"

Maya let the sketchbook slide back into its compartment.

Great-Uncle Harper rose from a table nearby. Today he wore a robe of sky blue. "Friends and colleagues," he cried, and all the grunting, screeching, rumbling, grating, and peeping stopped. Harper approached Maya and said, "Will you come and be presented?"

"What?" Everything she knew was seesawing inside her. One giant centipede, okay, she could deal with that. So much strangeness at once—

She teetered on her feet. Another spike of pain at her wrist, and she found her balance.

Egg-person, what are you doing to me?

Protecting you.

She swayed. Benjamin supported her this time.

One more tiny jab from the egg, and she blinked and steadied. She felt remote, her emotions calmed, packed up and put away. In the back of her mind, something was upset, but its alarm was soft and ignorable. She took a deep breath and let it out slowly. Okay. She could get through this. She could go crazy later.

Harper held out his hand, and she resettled her backpack on her shoulders, tightened the straps, and clasped hands with him. She wondered if the egg would shock him. It didn't. Maybe when she initiated contact instead of other people grabbing her, the egg let it happen. Then again, Gwenda and Benjamin had touched her without getting zapped.

"I want to explain your situation to the council," Harper said softly, so only she and the others nearby could hear. "Before we do that, may I have your answer? Will you let us make you part of our family?"

"I'm really confused right now," she said.

Harper turned his head, looked at what she was seeing. "Ah," he said. "I imagine so. It's been a long time since my wander year, but I recall that shock in a new situation. Can you take your mind back to a time before this confusion, and make yourself calm?"

Maya nodded, cupped her hand over the egg, moving her thumb over it. "I did. I think I'm there."

"Did you consider joining our family last night?"

"I did," she said.

"What was your conclusion?"

"Give me a moment."

She considered her problem one more time, from the state of egg-induced calm, and decided again that she needed a family that understood her new state, in addition the family she had been born into. She needed help with the *sissimi*, and she wanted to hang on to the magic. "Yes. I will join you." Her stomach clenched as she spoke. She was setting changes in motion, and she didn't know where they would lead.

Gwenda touched her arm. Benjamin smiled. Rowan frowned less.

"I can't—live with you and do what you all do, though. The special food, the classes, whatever it is you do I don't know about yet. I need to live with my own family. All right?"

"We would not expect you to. There are some things you should learn, and you'll need—" Harper broke off. "We need to negotiate. I will accept your yes as a yes, details to be decided upon later, to the benefit of all. Welcome to the family, cousin." He kissed her cheek and then the ring he had given her the night before.

He led her forward. All the beings had been waiting quietly. Harper nudged Maya to stand in front of him, and he rested his hands on her shoulders. "Council, may I present our new and accidental cousin? This is Maya, who through mishap became the bond-sister of one of the missing *sissimi*. Maya, will you show them the bonded one?"

Egglet, are you all right with being seen?

I don't know what "seen" is. Does it hurt?

No, she said, and wondered. She unbuttoned her cuff and turned back her sleeve, revealing her egg and its inner lights, glowing greens and blues with sparks of yellow.

Some of the creatures made noises. A few leaned forward and thrust parts of themselves toward her. She heard a hummingbird flutter: a fairy scudded through the air and hovered just above the egg, reached down a slender arm to touch Maya's skin, and left a tiny gold fingerprint. It was not the fairy she had seen before, the one who had started this chain of events that led to Maya standing here, in a hidden courtyard, surrounded by otherworlders. Its hair was pale instead of dark, and its features were different. It looked up at her face. Then it rose past her, gilt dust fluttering from its wings to settle across her shoulders. It sang something as it flew, then came to rest in a flower the size of a salad plate on one of the otherworldly shrubs.

A creature in a bubble reshaped itself so that it was taller, and said in a warm and melodious voice, "We all congratulate you on this auspicious addition to your family, Istar Harper, and we thank you for bringing these troubling new developments to our attention. We will continue to monitor activity along the portalways and inform each other of any suspicious traffic. Our cogitators will reflect on how to detect unsanctioned activity. Now, if it can be arranged, I am ready to return to my own portal."

Other creatures shifted position and added their own kinds of noises.

Harper said, "Thank you again, Maya. We have a lot to discuss, and time to discuss it. Excuse me while I see my guests out."

"Sure," she said.

He patted her and went toward a wide archway across the courtyard where most of the guests were heading.

One of the guests, a tall, slender woman in slate gray clothes with creases that looked as though they could cut, lingered, then came closer. She appeared almost human, though her skin was a grayish rose color, and her eyes were black without whites. A complicated black and silver scarf, looped in on itself so it looked like a cloth chain, wound around her shoulders and draped over her head, not quite concealing the fact that she was bald.

"I Ara-Kita Zizillian am," she said to Maya. "You, I, necessary to interact."

Maya looked at Gwenda, whose eyes were wide. Gwenda shook her head, as though she didn't know any more about this than Maya did.

Rowan stepped in front of Maya, facing Ara-Kita. "Traveler," he said. "Explain, please?"

"Keeper," she replied. "I Force am. Crimes division. Matter of the missing *sissimi*, information to pursue."

Rowan turned to Maya. "She's the police."

Maya took a deep breath. The egg-induced calm was still with her, so she didn't feel fear, just detached curiosity as she wondered whether she was about to be arrested. Where did portal people keep criminals?

"I've already told everything I know," Maya said, her voice level.

Ara-Kita nodded. "Heard. Wish embryo to interrogate."

"What?" Maya cupped her hand over the egg and stepped back.

"Only a moment it takes. Kita to it talks." The black and

silver scarf lifted a snakelike end, complete with a knob that could be a head, and swayed in the air, as though surveying Maya.

"Traveler Zizillian," Rowan said, "you speak with a member of my clan. Have you cleared this request with our *istar?*"

"Not formalized. Only a moment the questions take. No harm."

"Traveler," said Rowan, "I mean no disrespect. Come back when you have cleared this request, please."

The solid black eyes stared at Rowan, and the eyeless snake-head stilled to focus on him as well. After a concentrated moment, both heads bobbed. "Will. Kita greetings to little kin sends."

"Kin?" Maya said.

Ara blinked. She lifted a seven-fingered hand, and the snake-head lowered to rest on it. "Kita *sissimi* is," she said.

"A *sissimi!*" Maya stepped closer, staring and staring.

The knobby head came nearer, as though it stared, too, though there was nothing on it that looked like eyes. Silver was woven through its black length in intricate patterns. It did not look quite solid. Maya lifted her right hand toward it.

"Maya, wait," said Gwenda. "If you grant it permission to touch you, it may interact with you in ways we don't understand."

"But it's—is this what mine will look like?"

Ara said, "Every one different comes. Much on partner depends. But *sissimi-sissimi* without barriers can talk. If yours memories of the theft has, can mine tell."

Egg-person, do you want to talk to one of your own kind?

You are my only kind since I lost my other Other.

Maya closed her eyes. She felt as though a rosebud were opening in her chest, and at the same time, there was a sad taste in her mouth, the salt of tears. She stroked the egg. *Its partner says it is a being like you. I so much want to know more about you, and these people could tell us something. But what if it wants to hurt you?*

We are strong.

Maya smiled. *We don't know our strength yet.* Aloud, she said, "Pleased to meet you, Ara-Kita. I'd like to wait until Harper says it's okay before my *sissimi* talks to yours."

The snake relooped around Ara's neck and rested its head on top of her head. Ara bobbed again. "Will arrange." She turned and followed the others toward the far exit from the courtyard.

"Rowan, thanks," Maya said.

He huffed out a breath. "You're one of us now, whether I like it or not. We take care of our own. You've got a lot to learn before you meet travelers. Which is what I want to talk to Travis about, too. Come on." He headed toward the glass doors.

Maya looked at Benjamin, who smiled and shook his head. "He means well."

"Are you sure?" she asked, smiling.

"Pretty sure. Let's go find out if Travis is still here."

"So Rowan can give us some more orders?"

"Right," said Gwenda. "Hey. Are you hungry?"

Maya's stomach growled loudly. "Starving," she said.

"We can fix that."

Maya glanced at the half-consumed oddities on plates on the table.

"Naw, not that. It's all specific to who's eating it, and most of it's poison to us," said Benjamin. "Let's go to Rowan's."

NINETEEN

Rowan's apartment was different from Benjamin's. There was no tent drapery, no inlaid fretwork tables. The walls were pale yellow, the furniture upholstered in soft green. The living room looked like it belonged in a sitcom apartment: near normal, except for a bonsai tree on the coffee table and two potted pines in the corners. A small bookshelf held dictionaries and encyclopedias. A framed painting above the couch showed a stormy Oregon coast scene.

"This is where we bring outsiders," Gwenda said.

Travis sat on the couch, his head thrown back, napping. A dish holding nothing but crumbs was on the coffee table in front of him. Kallie worked at a nearby table, something that involved books, paper, and a quill pen. She set her quill down and smiled at Maya. "Are you officially one of us now?"

"I guess," said Maya.

"And Travis is officially *giri*. Two new people. That is so cool. Sometimes we get sick of each other."

Rowan came from an archway that led to the kitchen, which, from what Maya could see, looked showroom fresh. He carried a plate of sliced bread and oranges. "Sit," he said, waving her toward the couch. "Feed."

"Feed?" Maya settled beside Travis, and Rowan placed the plate in front of her. Her stomach growled again; it felt like a raging fire that needed fuel, but she hesitated to snatch food when there was something wrong with Rowan's verb.

"Help yourself," Benjamin said. He and Gwenda sat in chairs across the coffee table from the couch.

"Why do you have to be so snotty?" Maya asked Rowan.

He heaved a sigh. "You present problems."

"Not on purpose."

He slumped in an armchair near the couch. "Granted. Please. Have some food."

"Thanks." Maya ate a slice of bread in three bites. "What *is* this?" she asked as she reached for a second slice.

"Plum bread. Mother's specialty."

"It's delicious." She ate as slowly as she could manage, which wasn't very.

"And nutritious," said Rowan, "and freighted with *palta*. Kallie, did you send Travis to sleep?"

"Nope. He did that all by himself. He's like a champion sleeper. Two seconds and he's out."

"Travis, wake up, will you?" Rowan said, slightly louder.

Travis shuddered and sat up. "Huh?" He checked his watch. "Jeez Louise."

"How long can you give us?"

"Ten minutes."

"Good. I accept you both as necessary evils, and, since you're now part of our extended family, I need to explain some rules to you."

"Way to welcome them, Rowan," said Gwenda.

He glared at her and continued. "The first rule is silence about all you see in the house, but I guess Great-Uncle Harper took care of that, yes?"

"Hell, yeah," said Travis. "He ever do that to you? It's darned spooky."

"Rowan's never needed discipline," said Gwenda, "but I have. Silence is one of my least favorites."

"The second rule is study," said Rowan.

"You guys are like the psychos of the homeschool world, aren't you?" Travis said. "Except you come to regular school, too. How come you spend any time in regular school if you're going to spend your whole lives within thirty miles of this place? Couldn't you learn everything you need to know right here?"

"We would not learn how to socialize with our neighbors. That's important at every portal."

"Is that what you're supposed to be doing at school?" asked Travis. "I see Gwenda and Benjamin doing it, but Rowan, you *so* flunk. And I know from flunking."

Rowan straightened, brushed the hair away from his face, and gave Travis a full-throttle two-eyed glare. Maya, glad Rowan was focused elsewhere, finished off the oranges. She'd eaten half a loaf of plum bread—all he brought out. The gnawing in her stomach had gone down to nibbling.

"Yeah, yeah, glare all you like. Doesn't change the facts. So anyway, second rule, study. I don't have time to study. I'm already not studying for school as it is."

"Travis," Gwenda said, "why?"

"Why what?"

"Why don't you have time to study? Twyla said you were the smartest person in sixth grade. You did outside projects on Ancient Egypt and Ancient Greece. You built a Parthenon! She said you were planning to be an archaeologist. Then last year, what?"

Travis leaned back and crossed his arms over his chest. He frowned at the floor. "Last year," he said finally, "there was an accident." His gaze rose, met Maya's, met Rowan's, danced away. "Am I going to talk about this? I guess you need to know, or it'll be nag nag nag. My mom left when I was six, and me and my dad moved in with Oma and Opa. Oma raised me. She's the one got me studying other civilizations. Now that I know about this *giri* thing, I guess I understand she was interested in more than just what was going on on Earth.

"So Opa, also a good guy, but absentminded, last year he was driving Oma home from shopping, and he pulled out right in front of a truck—" He stopped and just breathed. No one spoke. "So, anyway, Opa never came home from that one, and Oma—so, Oma—" His hands closed into fists and he set them on his thighs. "She was hurt bad. She needs twenty-four-hour care, and we can't afford that. We have a couple nurses that come in during the day while Dad's at work and I'm at school. I'm supposed to be home at four to take over, and Dad gets home around seven and he helps. I've got a dog-walking business I take care of after Dad gets home. Oma tries not to be a burden, but she needs a lot of help, and she doesn't sleep a lot, and—" He jumped to his feet. "I've got to go."

He crossed the room and was out the door before anyone could speak.

"Community service," Gwenda said when they had sat in silence for a little while.

Benjamin sat up. "That's right. She's our *giri*, and he's a *giri* in training. Jemmy and Alira are studying eldercare, right? They could use some field practice."

"Aunt Raia's a nurse," Gwenda said. "She could probably help."

"Good thinking," Rowan said in a grumpy voice, "but let's solve all the world's problems later. Right now, Maya—"

"What am I supposed to be studying?" Maya asked.

"Well," said Rowan, "there's a whole curriculum for us, but I don't know how much of that will be useful to you. We don't know where your talents will be yet."

"Talents?"

"The skills we need to manage the portals, those are family things, and you probably won't have any of them, so you won't need energy theory and harmonics and voice lessons and personal tuning and group alignment, but you should learn some basic skills—"

"Do you mean, like, training me to work here? I don't

think—" Maya felt walls closing in on her. The egg heated. Red streaks crossed it.

"No," said Benjamin. "No, Rowan."

"What do you mean, no?"

"Did Great-Uncle Harper tell you you were supposed to inform Maya about new responsibilities?"

"He said tell her about our classes."

"You're not doing that," Benjamin said. "Maya, we study a lot of stuff. The older people teach the younger whatever they know. When someone shows a talent, they get focused teaching in that direction. What I think you could use, if you want, is a class in Kerlinqua, our special language, and maybe some classes in etiquette so you know acceptable ways to greet travelers."

"Joining your family doesn't mean I have to stay here forever, does it?"

"No, it doesn't."

"I'd like to learn more languages, and I'd like to know how to behave with—with travelers."

"Great," said Benjamin. "We could even start teaching you some of that at lunch. Here's what you should know: you don't have any family responsibilities yet. Just take care of yourself and learn what you can and tell us when you need help." He turned to Rowan. "Does that cover it?"

Rowan snorted and looked away.

"We have study rooms on the second story, where the Elders—and that includes everybody older than us—teach, and where we can practice. We can show you those later. For now, how about I walk you home?"

"I'd like that." Maya glanced at her watch and realized it was almost five. "I have to set the table. I'm so tired. I feel like I could sleep for a hundred years." Her stomach rumbled. "Um. After a snack."

When she and Benjamin stepped off the Janus House porch, Maya felt as though a weight lifted from her heart. She had so wanted to know all about the new neighbors. Now she just wanted to go home and pretend she was normal again.

"I know," said Benjamin, even though she hadn't said anything out loud. "It's a lot."

"You deal with things like that all the time."

"We're used to it. I bet it's big scary to you."

Maya scuffed her shoes on the grass. "Do you have any talents yet?"

"Nope. No special signs. I'm about average on a lot of stuff."

"Do you read minds? Any of you?"

He shook his head. "I know some travelers who have that talent, but none of the Earth Keepers do."

"That's a relief."

Her mother's car pulled into the driveway just as Maya unlocked the front door. Peter leaped out. "Who's your friend?"

"This is Benjamin, from next door," Maya said. "Benjamin, my brother Peter, my mom Liz."

"Nice to meet you, Ben," said Mom. She put down her briefcase and held out her hand.

He shook it, smiling. "My pleasure, Mrs. Andersen. Help you with the groceries?"

"That would be great," said Mom. She pointed her key fob at the car and beeped the back unlocked. Benjamin headed for the car, and Mom whispered, "What's with that family? Are they *all* that polite?"

"Not all of them," Maya whispered back. Then she headed toward the car to carry groceries, too.

"Do you know about creeks around here?" Peter asked Benjamin as they all carried plastic sacks of groceries into the house.

"Creeks?"

"Yeah, wild creeks where there are tadpoles and frogs and

things? I haven't seen one near here. Dad said there'd be a creek."

"Have you been to Westedge Park yet? There's a stream there. And there are restored wetlands out west of town, with nature trails in them."

"Great! Can you drive yet?"

"Peter!" cried Mom. Benjamin laughed. They put the grocery sacks on the table, and Peter went to the back door to let Sully in.

Sully rushed up to Maya and barked. She backed away from him, and he followed her, barking and barking, until she was trapped between the refrigerator and the stove.

"Sully! Stop that right now! Maya, do you have a steak in your pocket or something?" Mom asked.

"No!" *Egg-person,* she thought, *is there any way we can calm the dog?*

You trust this being? You like this being?

Yes.

"Sully, shut up," Peter yelled, but Sully ignored him. Benjamin looked worried, uncertain. His hands flexed as though he was about to do something, but he didn't follow through.

The egg thrummed, a sound below the threshold of hearing. Maya felt calmer and calmer as she felt the hum travel up the bones of her arm. It wasn't the same as when the egg calmed her during the council; this was more of a meditative state. Sully's frantic barks slowed. Finally he sat back with a yip and let his tongue loll out in a dog smile.

Maya crouched. "Hey, Sully," she murmured.

Wagging his tail, Sully came to lick her face. "Hey, boy. Hey." She hugged him and he woofed. Maya looked up at Benjamin. His face was still, his head tilted as though listening. He smiled then, and she felt better.

"What was the matter with you, you daft, darling dog?" Mom asked. "A moment of identity crisis? Did you forget you were a golden?"

Sully whined and went to sniff Benjamin's jeans. The dog accepted petting from everyone as Maya straightened. *Can we talk to animals?* she wondered.

That wasn't talk, answered the egg. *It was feel.*

Either way, it worked. Thanks, egg-person.

Welcome.

"Nice to meet you, Mrs. Andersen, Peter. I better get home now," Benjamin said.

"Benjamin, do you sing?" Mom asked suddenly.

"What?"

"Do you sing? We like to make music on Saturday nights. I was wondering if you'd care to join us."

He stood, his hand resting on Sully's head, and then a smile lit his face. "All of my family sings, ma'am, and I'd love to come if I can. I have to check with my parents."

"Bring anyone else you like, and if you have sheet music, that might help. If we don't know your music already, we'd like to learn."

"And bring your instruments," said Maya, remembering the weird-looking not-guitars and not-flutes she had seen them play.

"I'll tell them," he said. "Thanks, ma'am. Maya, see you tomorrow."

"'Night, Benjamin." Maya collected dishes and flatware and went to set the table.

TWENTY

In her room after supper, Maya painted a couple of pictures of the aliens she had seen in the courtyard that afternoon, even though she knew she was doing something Rowan wouldn't like. Benjamin had challenged Rowan on some of his rules. Maybe this was not a real rule, either. She wanted to paint another picture, but she was too tired to hold her eyelids open anymore.

She woke when something crackled in the air around her. Disoriented, she sat up, untangling her egg arm from its nest of pillows. The egg felt hot, and she was surrounded by a faintly gleaming pale blue bubble.

"Maya?" whispered someone. Two shadowy people

stood in her bedroom, one much taller than the other.

Maya blinked and checked the clock. Two A.M. She reached to switch on her bedside light, and the bubble moved with her, staying about a foot from her in all directions.

In the light, she saw that the shadows were Gwenda and Ara-Kita. "What?" she said. "What are you doing here?"

"I'm sorry we didn't let you know we were coming," Gwenda whispered. "We need to set up some kind of communication system for that." She went to the door and tapped the lock, then gestured through the air, singing a faint phrase of song that sounded like wind. "Okay, I set a silence ward so the rest of the house shouldn't be able to hear us," she said in a more normal tone. "Great-Uncle Harper cleared Ara-Kita to question your egg."

"At this time of night?" Maya rubbed her eyes.

"We wanted to make sure everyone else was asleep," said Gwenda. "Will you let us ask the little one questions?"

Egg? Maya thought.

Strong, the egg thought, but it sounded unsure.

"May I ask questions about Kita?" Maya said.

"Some I will answer," said Ara. "Please. What you know tell. What your partner knows tell."

"Okay," said Maya. She straightened the bedcovers, pulled

her knees up to her chest, and pointed toward the foot of the bed. The bubble moved with her. "Have a seat."

"Will you lower your shield?"

"*My* shield? My *shield?*" *Our shield, egglet?*

Ours. The egg tensed, and then, with a *plink*, the bubble vanished.

"Thanks," said Ara-Kita. She sat at the foot of Maya's bed. "Strong one, so early a shield to make. *Svelala.*" She smiled, flashing pointed teeth.

Kita lifted its head-knob and flowed through the air toward Maya, though most of its body stayed looped over Ara's shoulders and head. It paused about a foot from Maya's face.

"Your arm lift? Your *sissimi* show?" Ara said.

Maya raised her left arm and slid her sleepshirt's sleeve back to uncover the egg. Yellow, green, and rosy lights darted across its surface.

"Ah," said Ara, "so pretty. Good health."

Kita neared Maya's wrist, approaching slowly, its head weaving. It paused a couple of inches away.

"Ready?" Ara asked.

Maya bit her lip and nodded.

The black head dipped to touch her egg. Shock jolted

through Maya, tingled out the ends of her fingers and toes. Her hair crackled with electricity.

And then, a honey-sweet flow, a caress, a mother-child touch, the brush of feathered wingtips. A high, lilting tune. No words, but a whistle of lifetimes passing each other, a two-way street with near-instant traffic going in both directions.

Maya's mouth was wide. She stared at Ara, whose face was stretched, wide-mouthed and wide-eyed, too.

A final kiss of farewell. Kita lifted its head from Maya's egg. Maya gulped breath. Tension she hadn't even been aware of holding ran out of her. Ara's shoulders slumped and her head dropped forward. "Oh," she gasped. "More than I knew."

Oh, oh, oh!

Egg-person! Are you all right?

I am so happy!

Maya leaned back against her headboard, her arms and legs sagging like a marionette's whose strings had been cut. *Happy?*

I've learned so much. We will be able to—

Ara straightened. Her pale green tongue darted out of her mouth and licked her lips. "Oh, so much help! The taste-smell of the Rimi-thief, the images of Krithiworks. Rimi-thief the other thieves knew, all together on Krithi trained. We them will find. Blessings, blessings! You I thank, and you I thank, Maya-Rimi."

Rimi? thought Maya.

Maya, thought the egg.

"Rimi," Maya said aloud, and smiled.

* TWENTY-ONE *

Friday, Maya found herself drowsing through school almost as much as Travis did. Rimi hummed on her wrist, thinking thoughts too quick for Maya to catch, full of satisfaction and excitement.

She and Travis both sat with the Janus House kids at lunch. Benjamin had brought an extra lunch for each of them. Maya ate her own lunch, the lunch Benjamin brought her, and everything anybody else didn't. The Janus House kids taught them a few Kerlinqua words.

After school, they all set out together. "I think I better actually go home today," Maya said. "For one thing, I need a nap. And I don't want Mom and Dad thinking I'm spending too much time at your house."

"You have to start learning—" Rowan began.

"Not today."

"You go, Maya." Twyla pumped her fist.

Maya smiled at her.

They were halfway home when an older girl in gypsy clothes ran up to them on the sidewalk. "We need you," she said to the Janus House kids. "And you," she said to Maya. She looked at Travis. "Not sure about you."

"What happened, Alira?" asked Rowan.

"The Force found the *sissimi* thief and brought him to the house."

In an upstairs apartment outfitted like a hospital room with interesting artwork and no television, Chikuvny Boy lay on a bed under a warm yellow light. A middle-aged, dark-skinned woman in a raspberry dress hovered over him. She tipped something into his mouth from a small, steaming teapot with a long crooked spout.

Harper and the Tree Sisters and Ara-Kita were all in the room when the kids arrived.

"She found him in the park near the middle school," Raspberry Woman said. "He was very ill, hiding, but Ara-Kita scented him. I don't recognize his origin, nor does she."

Chikuvny Boy's breath rattled in and out. His eyes were closed; the sockets looked bruised. His ruddy hair was flattened against his skull, damp and dark. His skin was even paler than it had been when Maya had seen him two days earlier, and slick with sweat. The freckles across his nose and cheeks looked like dark stars in a white sky.

Rimi was agitated on Maya's wrist. *My other Other. My other Other!*

"I don't know how to treat him, since I don't know where he's from." Raspberry Woman bathed the boy's forehead with a wet cloth. "Our usual remedies are as likely to harm as help."

"Maya," Harper said gently, and Benjamin led her over to the sick boy.

Help! cried the egg. The blue bubble sprang up around Maya, reached toward the boy on the bed. It pushed out toward him and stubbed itself on his arm, unable to enclose him. *No,* whispered Rimi. *He is no longer mine.* A melody of mourning ran through Maya's mind. Rimi's shield dropped. Maya pressed her hands to her stomach, trying to push back the pain.

Chikuvny Boy opened his eyes and stared into Maya's.

He sucked in a gurgling breath. "Does it hurt you now?" he whispered.

"No." She held up her wrist where he could see it. He stared at the lights shining from the egg.

"Good. Beautiful." He lifted a hand toward the egg, dropped it. "Where?" He looked around without moving his head.

"These are the people who know about the portals," she said.

"Good," he gasped. "She will be safe. Good."

"Child," said Harper to the boy, "we are trying to help you. Can you tell us who you are and where you are from?"

The boy took some more rattling breaths. "My name is Bikos Serani." Pause. "My home is Minsla."

Harper glanced at the others. They all shook their heads. "We don't know where that is."

"It has no real portals. Only Krithi portals."

"Krithi portals!"

Maya hunched her shoulders. Everybody in the room looked mad or frightened, and the air felt tight.

"Is there no way we can get a doctor from your world?" Raspberry Woman asked.

"It is too late," Bikos said, his voice fading on the last

word. "Only to know she is safe. That is enough." He lifted his hand again, and this time Maya reached across, set the egg under his fingertips.

He gasped, and she gasped. *She fell into being who he had been—*

He huddled under a large, battered, plastic half bubble while rain from an amber sky drummed down on the clear rounded surface above him, and on the ground, sending up splashes of thin red mud. Wrapped in a ragged cloth, his toes in the cold water, he watched small dead things float by.

Then he was surrounded by tall, narrow people with lemon chiffon-, key lime pie-, and blueberry yogurt-colored skin, their snaky, knobby hair-vines darker colors, their clothes bumpy and strange, with parasols—or something made of webbing stretched over jointed frameworks—moving behind their heads. Their eyes were wide and pale and jeweled, and some had two sets of eyes, one above the other.

The blueberry yogurt one knelt near him, tipped back the bubble, and held out slender arms that ended in hands with doubled fingers. He shrank back. The alien took him anyway. It hugged Bikos to its hard, bumpy chest. It felt so warm in the cold rain, and it smelled like wet leather and fried rice. The two parasols—large webbed batwing hands—reached forward over its shoulders to shield Bikos from the rain.

The alien carried him through a red rip in the sky. A painful twisting in the gut as he went through, a clawing in the chest as his last breath fled and there was no air to take another breath, a ringing in the ears, but then, out the other side, a different world.

The sun shone hot here, and the buildings were sand-colored domes, the plants wispy and thin leaved, brownish orange and dark plum purple. The knobby-haired people carried him inside and underground and put him in a warm, weedy-smelling pond with a tray of food floating on its surface. One came into the water with him and fed him.

Everyone was similar to those who had saved Bikos— varied colors, batwing hands, knobbly dreads, beautiful eyes. They fed him and shared comforts with him he had never known before, warmth and luxury and music. They trained him to run and taught him other skills. He didn't know what they wanted. He didn't ask. For the first time in his memory, his stomach was full enough all the time, and he was not cold. One of the people was his special caretaker, and she was always nice to him; he adored her.

When they asked him if he would do a thing for them, of course he said he would.

"We have to send you to a place we cannot go. There's something there we need. It is the seed of a friend who will protect you and love you. If you can claim it, you will always have a friend with you."

Yes, he said. They showed him images in the air of places, taught him the safe ways to run through them, and told him what he would need to do.

They showed him the portal. A red rip in the sky.

Again it hurt to go through, but not as much as it had the first time. He had strength now, and hunger wasn't clawing at him.

He stood inside a warm, steaming glass house full of sprawling, muscular vines. Glowing, egg-shaped fruit dangled between large velvety purple and blue leaves. He reached up, took a fruit ("Make sure you get a glowing one; the others are not ripe," they had told him), and snapped it from its stem. All the leaves surged in the glass house. Other fruits still on the branches trembled, and vines squirmed. Long, curl-tipped tendrils reached for him.

The fruit's steady yellow glow changed as he took it. Blue and green lights glowed under its velvet skin. He tucked it inside his shirt, felt the first swell of loving-kindness from the one who would now be his absolutely, and he ran.

Friend.

Maya knew that feeling, something you could wrap up in, safe and warm. She felt again the break that happened at separation, Bikos's loss as he pressed the egg against Maya's wrist to save its life, the gaping empty place that tore through Maya the afternoon she went to the hospital to visit Stephanie and learned she had died that morning, while Maya was in school.

Bikos knew he would kill the egg if he kept it. He couldn't do that to a friend.

Maya hadn't been able to do anything to stop Stephanie's death from coming, but she had rescued Rimi.

"Maya?" Gwenda touched her shoulder.

She blinked. Chill touched her wet cheeks.

A roomful of strangers stared at her.

Bikos stared at her, too.

The edges of his mouth curved up into a tiny smile.

His hand slid off the egg.

His eyes fell shut, and he stopped breathing.

* TWENTY-TWO *

Weeping raged through her. She dropped to the floor. She ripped open her pack and pulled out her new sketchpad, grabbed a big soft pencil, and drew and drew. Drew the bubble with rain streaming down over it, the clouded sky, the water flowing past with small dark things in it. Drew the face of the alien caretaker, with the wing-hands up behind it; drew other faces of those Bikos had seen on the sandy planet, some with four eyes, some with two; drew their ropes of hair and knobby clothes and wing-hands, spread or collapsed, fanning gently or shading them from the sun.

The pool where Bikos had first tasted a special root only *Inkept* people could have.

The warm, sandy pit where they had set him to play with their young, games of grab-the-shiny-first-and-curl-away-from-others—how he longed for his own wing-hands to protect him! And muscular hair vines to tickle and snatch and signal moods. The other children, not Krithi, who were being trained to run, to steal. Other children like him who lacked wing-hands and hair-vines.

The glass house with the *sissimi* vines; the big, splayed, many-fingered leaves; the glowing fruit dangling within reach, asking to be picked.

She sketched across each page, clotted it with details, then ripped it out and went to the next, sharpening her pencil as it wore down. All the while, another feeling flooded her—the loss the egg had felt, this second tearing away of its first twin.

She cried, too, for Stephanie, so tired of all the if onlys. If only Steph were here—well, she wasn't. She wasn't. Maya had to do this without her.

She drew a huddle of three people facing inward, many-fingered hands laced together, wing-hands fluttering around their heads.

The red rip in the sky—though with pencil, she couldn't show the color. No circle of six had created it; she looked through memory at the times Bikos had seen it. No special cavern, no songs, no markings on the ground. Oh. There was a machine, both times—she outlined it, and its two operators.

She couldn't draw how Bikos had felt when they picked him up to carry him away through the stomach-twisting rip, but she still felt it, the fear and hope as he left behind everything he had ever known.

She drew a boy wrapped in the embrace of three of these people. She didn't know if they were men or women, only that they closed in around him and made him feel warm and safe.

She drew until her pencil was nothing but a nub. She cried the whole time, sniffling, sobbing, scrubbing her nose on her arm.

She looked up at last and found Rowan and Gwenda and Benjamin close around her, like the three people huddled around the boy in the last picture. Across from her sat Harper and some others. They were studying her pictures, murmuring to each other.

Gwenda handed her a big snowy handkerchief.

She wiped her face and blew her nose, then she climbed unsteadily to her feet and went to the bed.

Bikos lay with his hands folded across his stomach. She touched his hand. It was only faintly warm, and already stiff.

She looked across at Raspberry Woman. The medic's eyes were wide and wet. "I wish I could have helped him."

Maya sniffled. She stroked the egg down her cheek over her tears. She fetched her sketchpad and looked for a blank page, but she had used them all. She reclaimed one of the drawings and found a different pencil in the outer pocket of her backpack. Resting the sketchpad's stiff cardboard against the bed, she placed the loose page facedown, and on its back she drew Bikos's abandoned body, the resting peace of his empty face.

Her sobs stopped. The flow of line from her brain through her hand and out the end of the pencil calmed her.

Gwenda's hand rested warm on her shoulder. Maya's fingers slowed. She lifted the pencil tip from the paper and closed her eyes.

Stephanie and Bikos were gone. Not coming back. Miracles were all around Maya, and they couldn't stop death.

✴ TWENTY-THREE ✴

"Maya, are you all right?" her father asked at the supper table.

Maya had gotten home just in time for curfew. After . . . everything, she had curled up in a big cushiony chair in Benjamin's apartment, communing with the egg, sharing sadness. Gwenda had brought her more vinegar soup. At first, her stomach tightened, but then it growled, and she ate and was comforted. Then she felt terrible for letting go of her sadness and betraying Bikos's memory.

The moon-pendant Tree Sister sat beside her and stroked her back, saying nothing.

Benjamin finally sat down beside Maya and gripped her

hand. "You saved his friend. That was what he wanted."

Rimi's sorrow tasted of salt and peppermint.

Eventually, Maya got up and washed her face and came home. The Janus House people had kept all her drawings except the last one, which she had tucked into her backpack. She had set the table, though it took her longer than usual; she kept zoning out, waking up to see her hand holding a spoon or a napkin. With a start, she would remember her task and continue it.

Candra had been on dinner duty, and she had made spaghetti and meatballs, garlic bread, and salad, one of Maya's favorites.

The other kids had talked about their day already. Maya had been trying to figure out what to say when it was her turn.

She blinked and looked down at her plate, where she had used her fork to drag the spaghetti into spirals with clear centers, like the ones in the picture Benjamin had drawn of his family.

"Just sad," she said.

Mom sighed and said, "New sad or old sad?"

"Both," said Maya. Her stomach rumbled, and she remembered she was eating for two. She ate a bite of spaghetti. Her appetite woke up. Again. She bolted her food.

"Whoa," said her father. "Maybe you should chew before you swallow?"

"What's the new sad?" asked Candra as Maya reached for seconds.

Maya didn't know how to answer. She couldn't tell her family she had watched someone die. They would want to know details.

She glanced around the table. All of them were staring at her. She loved them so much, and they were receding from her. A wall of secrets closed her off from them now.

"Are your new friends making you sad?" Peter asked.

"Kind of. Not them, really, just some things about them."

"Gwenda's little brother, Bran, is in my class," Peter said.

"He is? I didn't even know she had a brother."

"He's weird." Peter munched the middle out of a piece of garlic bread and held the crust under the table for Sully.

"What kind of weird?" asked Dad.

"He hardly talks at all, and he eats weird food, and he sits alone all the time."

"Benjamin and Gwenda were like that, too, but I sat with them anyway," Maya said.

"Did you tell us their last names?" Mom asked.

"Um, maybe not. Janus, Porta, Gates? There might be others. Those are the ones I've met," said Maya.

"I've got a Janus girl in one of my classes," Dad said.

Candra said, "These kids, last name Janus? Porta? Gates? Come to think of it, one of the guys on the school paper was talking about doing an exposé on them. Their family has lived in Spores for decades. They're ultrapolite. They all do their homework on time. They don't join anything; they don't make friends; they don't participate in extracurriculars; they never come to games. He figures they must be hiding bodies in the basement, or maybe they have weird religious practices. I'm getting excited just thinking about it. Peter, make friends with that kid Bran. Try to find out about his home life. Maya, you're the only person I've heard of who's been inside the building. What can you tell us about what's behind their doors?"

Maya shrugged. "Apartments," she said. "A central courtyard with cool plants in it. And man, can they cook."

"I can't be*lieve* they're that boring! There must be more to it!" Candra said.

"That's all I got," said Maya.

Candra narrowed her eyes. "You're hiding something. I'm going to dig it out. Just you wait, missy!"

"Color me scared," Maya said. She hoped Candra thought she was kidding.

* TWENTY-FOUR *

Maya woke in the middle of the night and didn't know why.

Where her Idaho window used to be, all she saw was dark.

She turned her head. Faint orange light from the street-lamp came in through her Oregon window and printed a tangerine shape on the ceiling.

She glanced at the clock. Three A.M. The house was silent.

What had awakened her? A sound? She struggled to sit up. Her left arm was tangled in pillows.

The egg! It was hot against her wrist, and pulsing. Throbbing.

She turned her ring three times, then sat up and switched on the bedside lamp.

Light flared by her bookcase: a flickering sheet of orange, red, and yellow, along with a wash of *chikuvny* scent. Gwenda stepped out of the lightstorm, yawning into her hand. She had on a blue flannel nightgown and looked way too ordinary for someone who had just appeared out of thin air.

"Is it now?" Gwenda whispered. She had a basket over her arm.

"I think so," Maya whispered.

Gwenda took a stick out of the basket and traced the walls of the room with its tip, writing symbols in the air. She scribed toward the ceiling, then the floor. She sang pieces of melody. "Okay," she said. "I've warded us, even stronger than I did last night. Nobody can hear what goes on in this room or come in until I take the wards down. Even if I have to go for help, we should be okay."

"Thanks," Maya said.

Maya lifted her left wrist and stared at it. Gwenda settled next to her on the bed, staring, too.

The egg lay on top of Maya's skin now, like something superglued to her wrist, no longer under her skin. Colors streaked and swirled and exploded over its soft shell. She touched it. Velvet soft, a pulse of heat against her fingertip, a burst of butter yellow. For a moment she couldn't breathe. Sweat wet her forehead and scalp, soaked her back. Something . . . something . . .

A tiny cracking noise.

Hatching.

What was she supposed to do?

Panicked, she stared at Gwenda.

What if Rimi died?

"It'll be all right," Gwenda whispered. "Help is just a short step away."

"I should have brought food," Maya said. "I didn't even think. What if it's hungry? What does it eat? Why didn't I ask Ara-Kita what to do when I had the chance?"

"*Sissimi* can get along on all worlds, as long as they connect to someone local. It'll be all right, Maya."

Crack!

She couldn't move.

The eggshell split. A tiny green tendril poked out. Then another, and another, and another. They waved in the air, little flat ribbons of green, dancing. Curling and straightening, like baby fingers reaching for the moon.

Maya held her right index finger above the green ribbons. One wavered toward her finger, touched it. The faintest flick, the touch of a feather. It curled around her finger.

The other ribbons reached for her finger, too. Then more and more of them came out of the egg, longer ones, wider ones. They wound around her fingers, locked her fingers together, and bound her right hand to her left wrist. They were warm and damp, stretchy and superstrong, tight, but not tight enough to hurt.

Oh, man. Her arms were locked together. This was going to be hard to hide.

So many ribbons came out of the egg that her right hand looked like it was mummy-wrapped in narrow bands of green. She couldn't figure out how the egg had held all those ribbons.

Finally a small green lump came out of the egg, the base of all the ribbons, and her right hand broke free, taking the lump with it. Her hand was tied up tight to itself, but it wasn't connected to her left wrist anymore.

The eggshell darkened to gray. It shredded and fell off, then powdered and blew away like ashes.

Maya flexed her left wrist. There was a pale pink oval of

skin on it in the middle of her summer tan. Her wrist worked again, though, and it didn't hurt.

She sighed and looked at what used to be her right hand.

The lump sat on top of her fingers. All its streamers wriggled, tensing and untensing around her hand. Some unwound and reached up and down and out.

It looked like nothing she'd ever seen before. Had Kita ever looked like this?

"Rimi. What are you?" she whispered.

Rimi.

"I know that. What else are you?"

Rimi thought a smile at her, and Maya had to laugh.

Gwenda held out a finger. Emerald ribbons lifted from Maya's hand and danced toward Gwenda's.

"Hey, Rimi," Gwenda crooned, edging her finger closer. Ribbons wrapped around Gwenda's finger, reached past it to envelop her hand.

"Wait a second!" Gwenda tried to pull away, but Rimi wouldn't release her. "Oh! She's so strong! Let go, Rimi!"

Look what I caught. The *sissimi*'s little-girl voice sounded proud.

Maya laughed again. She couldn't help it. She was sitting in her bedroom after three A.M. with her drawing hand mummy-wrapped by her alien friend, who had just caught her human friend and wouldn't let go.

"Maya?" Gwenda said.

Can I keep it? asked Rimi.

"Maya? Tell her to let go. Maya?"

* TWENTY-FIVE *

"Rimi, we need to talk," Maya said. Gwenda had managed to peel off the green ribbons that bound her to Maya—but only because Rimi let her, after a few minutes where the *sissimi* held on so tight Maya actually wondered if she and Gwenda would be welded together for life. "You can't live on my hand."

I know. There is much more of you I need to learn. Emerald ends of ribbons rose wavering in the air, flickering like snakes' tongues. *What next?*

"If you're going to stay on me, I need you someplace I can cover with clothes. My back?"

Where is that?

Maya frowned and tried to reach her back with her right hand. Her nightgown got in the way. Finally she slid her green-wrapped hand inside the neckline behind her head. She felt shifting on her hand, heard faint crackly noises, then felt stripes walking down her back. A final tickle against her fingers, and Rimi was away. Maya rested her freed hands on her thighs and flexed her fingers, smiling at the return of independent function, as many thin warm things moved around on her back.

"Disturbing," said Gwenda, watching the back of Maya's nightgown.

"What does it look like?" Maya rose and went to the mirror. She turned her back and tried to peer over her shoulder. Things lifted and shifted under her nightgown like a nest of baby snakes. Several green ribbons rose up from the neck of her gown and eased into her hair, wove through it. "Rimi?"

I need to know you.

A wave of tiredness washed over Maya. She went to the bed and sat down, carefully, then lay on her stomach. "Can I put a blanket over you?" she asked Rimi.

That is fine. You cannot hurt me. I am too strong.

"Is it okay?" Gwenda asked.

"Yes."

Gwenda worked the top sheet and blanket out from under Maya and covered her with them. "Go to sleep," she said. "I'll get some blankets and food from my place and come right back. I'll watch tonight."

"Thank you," Maya murmured, and then, despite the nest of flat, wriggling snakes on her back, she fell asleep.

"Maya?" someone murmured in her ear.

Maya groaned. She was lying on her stomach. Usually she slept on her back. She felt so hungry!

A sliding sound near her head, and the smell of soup. Maya groaned again and pushed herself up. Gwenda, huddled in a puffy green quilt, was sitting by Maya's bed. She held up a small cauldron full of steaming vinegar soup.

Maya turned over and reached for the cauldron. It was heavier than she expected. Gwenda gave her a wooden spoon, and she ate. When she finished, she looked at the clock. Five A.M. "What happened?" she asked.

"We both fell asleep," Gwenda said. "I set my inner alarm for four thirty, though, so we can tidy things up before you go back to your regular life. Where's the *sissimi*? Last time I saw it, it was on your back, but now—"

"Huh?" Maya reached behind her and felt her back. It felt flat and normal. "Huh? Rimi!"

Here, thought Rimi, only Maya couldn't tell where *here* was. *Here* felt like everywhere.

"Where are you?"

I am with you.

Maya pushed back her nightgown sleeves, searching for signs of green. She felt the back of her neck. She got out of bed and looked in the mirror, lifted the gown and looked at her legs. No green anywhere. "Are you sure, Rimi? Where did you go?"

I finished my explorations and took my next form, thought Rimi.

"What's that?" Maya asked.

Something dark moved beside her. The bedside lamp threw her shadow across the floor and the dresser, and it looked like her shadow rose up, only it stayed where it was, too. Its twin rose to hover next to Maya, taking a more Maya-like shape, still attached at the soles of her feet. *Here*, said Rimi. *I can stay with you safely, and no one will notice. And if something bad comes—*

The shadow swelled suddenly and surrounded her. It shimmered, cleared, and hardened. She felt like she was inside a giant, transparent pill capsule. She flattened her hand against the inside of the shell, which was smooth and slick. "Rimi! This is you?"

One way of being me. The capsule melted and the shadow settled into the outline of her other shadow again. *I have others.*

"Wow." Maya plopped down on her bed, staring at her shadow. Companion. Collector. Protector.

Collector of what? *Shri?* Stealth and spying . . . she would worry about that later.

Friend. Friend who wasn't going anywhere without her.

"Wow," said Gwenda. "Not like Kita. No wonder there weren't any pictures in that darned book."

"I can draw that," Maya said.

Gwenda smiled. "Yes, you can."

Gwenda undid the wards and packed up everything she had brought with her. "Call me the same way if you need any more help," she said.

"Thank you so, so much," said Maya.

"You're welcome. This is a part of my work I enjoy. Congratulations on your new companion. I guess I should say that to both of you."

Thank you, friend.

Maya spoke Rimi's words aloud, then said, "Rimi, how am I going to feed you now?"

I can feed myself. I can eat light. I can eat dust. I can eat anything I touch.

"But you'll be selective, right?"

I will only eat things that taste good.

"Uh-oh."

TWENTY-SIX

Saturday was a day to work on cleaning, unpacking, and setting up the house more, Dad decreed. He went to Home Depot and bought screens for the upstairs windows, plus picture hangers and bookshelves. They went through the house, fixing one room at a time.

"Tonight we're having Music Night," Mom said midway through the morning, "so I'm going to bake now."

"Music Night," Candra said, and stuck out her tongue.

"If you honestly have better things to do, go and do them," said Dad. "I'd rather have you absent than here and unpleasant."

"I invited the neighbors," Mom said. "Maya, if you want to practice, I'll excuse you from cleaning duty."

Maya put down her cleaning rag, washed her hands, and sat at the piano for the first time in the new house. She played "She'll Be Comin' Round the Mountain," and she cried. (Stephanie had always sung, "She'll be driving six white unicorns when she comes.") She played "Long Black Veil," and she cried, remembering it was Steph's favorite. ("First-person ghost! How many songs are first-person ghost? How cool is that?") She played "Wind and Rain," about a girl whose jealous sister threw her in the river, and a fiddler found her corpse and made a fiddle out of her breastbone, and Maya didn't cry, because before she got to the really sad part, Candra shoved her off the piano bench and said, "Stop it with the weeping!" and played "Papa's on the Housetop" and "The City of New Orleans" and "Angelina Baker," all happy or silly songs that Maya hadn't heard since last winter. She found herself smiling, even though these were all songs Stephanie had loved, too.

Were you done with the crying part? Rimi asked. *If you want more, we can move her.*

We can? Maya thought. *Oh, dear. I bet we can. Let's not!* She went to the art supplies cupboard and took down another sketchbook.

"Didn't you take one of those a couple days ago?" Dad asked.

"I used it all up."

He opened his mouth, shut it. Opened it, shut it again. Finally he said, "May I see what you've been working on?"

She froze.

She couldn't show him. The sketches were at Janus House, being studied. Harper had told her the people with the wing-hands were Krithi, all right, and somebody said the details (the steaming ponds, the clothing, the knobbly hair-vines, the floating trays of food) were all documented parts of Krithi home-planet culture. Other aspects of the pictures weren't familiar to anyone, and they were all interested.

And Rowan had said— But Rowan wasn't always right.

"I left most of them at Benjamin's," Maya said.

"Why?"

"His family loves my art."

"So do we," said her father. "Do you have anything you can show me?"

"I think—yes, I do." She ran upstairs and brought down the color pictures she had done the night Gwenda came to dinner—the family dinner, the portal team summoning the gate, the sketches of her egg. She handed them to her father. He laid them all out on the living room floor.

Mom came from the kitchen and studied Maya's pictures with Dad. Peter wandered from one to the next. Candra joined them.

"This one of the family is excellent," said Dad. "What are these other pictures?"

"Are you telling another story?" asked Peter. "I miss the stories."

He had been the biggest fan when Maya and Stephanie drew and wrote together. She had showed him those pictures and told him the stories Stephanie had told her. He loved them.

"Yes. It's another story," Maya said.

"Who are these guys?" He pointed to a picture of the portal, all rags and ribbons of color, with people, their arms outstretched, black silhouettes against the light.

"They're dancing around a fire on another world," Maya said.

"And then what happens?"

"I don't know. I don't know how to put it together."

"What's this one?" He pointed to a picture of the egg.

"Just pretty colors."

"I think it's an alien egg," he said.

Maya startled, then smiled. Rimi feathered laughing touches around her ankles.

"Oh, Maya, they're beautiful," her mother said. "Honey, it's great to see you doing something new." She hugged Maya. Maya let herself melt into this feeling of being enveloped in uncomplicated love. Since Stephanie's death, every hug from her parents had had a question in it: *Are you over it yet?*

"What about this one?" Peter asked.

Mom released Maya, and both of them turned to look.

Lying on the floor was Maya's pencil sketch of Bikos after he died.

"Where did you get that?" she demanded.

Peter hunched his shoulders. "In your backpack."

"How many times have I told you—"

"I wanted to see more of the story," he told the floor. "It doesn't make sense yet."

"Maya," said her father, "who is this?"

She opened her mouth and nothing came out. A taste of licorice crossed her tongue. She remembered Harper striking silence into her.

"Is this boy sleeping?" her mother asked.

"He looks dead," said Peter.

Maya used the silence to think. "Sometimes people die in stories," she said. She turned the picture over. On the back was a picture of the three Krithi surrounding the boy.

"Wow," said Dad. "What's happening here?"

Even if she had wanted to tell them, she knew she couldn't. "What does it look like?"

"Aliens," said Peter, "and a human boy. And it's raining. They have wings? Can they fly?"

"I don't think so. I can't tell the story," Maya said, "not anymore. I needed Steph for that. I can't tell it, but I can draw it."

"Well, it's terrific," said her father. "Keep doing it, and take all the sketchbooks you want." He kissed her cheek.

Maya took the new sketchbook upstairs and sat on the bed, thinking about silence. Harper had tapped her tongue, but he hadn't touched her drawing hand. Maybe the wall of secrets didn't have to be so high, even if her family didn't know she was drawing her own story.

That night, Benjamin and Gwenda and Rowan and Twyla and Kallie and Bran and a lot of other people filed over from Janus House, most of them carrying their own chairs, some with instrument cases slung over their shoulders or strapped to their backs, some with plates of sliced fruit bread or cake, one with a pitcher of what looked like juice. "Good evening," said Great-Uncle Harper when Mom opened the door to them. This time he was wearing a turquoise business suit. Maya wondered if that was his idea of normal dress. "We understand there's music here tonight?"

"Yes, yes! Come in, come in!" Mom opened the door wide. "We're so glad to have you!"

"We are delighted your family moved into the Spring House," said Harper. "I'm Harper Janus, and these are my folk."

Mom smiled wide. "I'm Liz Andersen, and these are *my* folk. I think you know Maya already. This is my son, Peter, and my husband—where is my husband? Drew, come meet the neighbors!"

Dad came down from upstairs, where he had been looking for the box they had packed their sheet music in. "Hoo, boy," he said. "This is wonderful! I don't know if the living room's big enough."

"Doesn't matter. There's lots of lawn," said Harper. "Just open the windows so we can hear each other, and we'll do fine."

"Whoa," said Candra, who had just come from the kitchen. Chocolate stained one corner of her mouth. She must have been taste-testing the brownies, Maya thought. She smiled. "Howdy, folks! I'm Candra!"

Gwenda joined Maya. "Do you know where Travis lives?" she whispered. "Maybe we could get him and his grandmother."

"Don't know yet," said Maya. "Maybe next week."

I can find him, Rimi thought.

Not right now, Maya thought.

"Hey, Bran," Peter said. "Wanna meet my dog? He's in the backyard."

"Sure."

"The big question now is, do we know any of the same songs?" Dad said. "We're folk song enthusiasts. How about you?"

"Music is our life," said Harper. "We embrace it all."

"Let's get set up. Take the refreshments on back to the kitchen, all right?"

People smiled and nodded, and other people put what chairs could fit in the living room, and the rest on the porch and the lawn. People took their instruments out of the cases and tuned them. Up close, some looked like normal fiddles and guitars, but others—

"What is that, please?" Maya asked a dark-haired boy.

"A balalaika," he said.

"Maya," said her father, when everyone had settled, "you pick the first song and let's see what happens."

"Let's sing 'I'll Fly Away,'" she said.

She had never heard a choir more beautiful than the one

she heard then. The voices were so rich and strong she wished she could dip a brush in them and paint the music. Harmony and counterpoint wove through the main melody. She felt knots inside her untie. The music carried sadness away.

Magic, she thought, and she joined her voice to the others'.

NINA KIRIKI HOFFMAN is the author of a number of adult and YA novels, as well as hundreds of short stories. Her works have been finalists for the World Fantasy, Mythopoeic, Theodore Sturgeon, Philip K. Dick, and Endeavour Awards. Her first novel, *The Thread That Binds the Bones*, won a Stoker Award, and her short story "Trophy Wives" won a Nebula Award in 2009.

Nina does production work for *The Magazine of Fantasy & Science Fiction*. She also works with teen writers. She lives in Eugene, Oregon, with several cats and many strange toys and imaginary friends.

You can learn more about her work at www.ofearna.us/books/hoffman.html.